Cultivating Hope

Homesteading on the Great Plains

Cultivating Hope

Homesteading on the Great Plains

Linda K. Hubalek

Butterfield Books, Inc.
Lindsborg, Kansas

Cultivating Hope
© 1998 by Linda K. Hubalek

Printed in the United States of America

For details and order blanks for the *Butter in the Well* series, the *Trail of Thread* series, and the *Planting Dreams* series, please see page 111 in the back of this book. If you wish to contact the publisher or author, please address to Butterfield Books, Inc., PO Box 407, Lindsborg, KS 67456-0407. Each book is $9.95, plus $3.00 s/h for the first book ordered and $.50 for each additional book.

Consulting Editor: Susan Novak
Cover Design: Lightbourne Images
Cover photo of Emily, Gilbert, and Oscar Johnson, circa 1884.
Photos courtesy of Don Johnson and Lester E. Johnson.

Publisher's Cataloging-in-Publication
   (Prepared by Quality Books, Inc.)

   Hubalek, Linda K.
   Cultivating hope : homesteading on the Great Plains /
   Linda K. Hubalek. -- 1st ed.
   p. cm. -- (Planting dreams series; no. two)
   Includes bibliographical references.
   Preassigned LCCN: 98-70571
   ISBN 1-886652-12-0
   1. Swedish Americans--Kansas--Saline County--Fiction.
   2. Frontier and pioneer life--Kansas--Saline County--
   Fiction. 3. Homestead law--United States--Fiction.
   4. Saline County (Kan.)--Fiction.   I. Title.
   PS3558.U19C85 1998   813'.54
                                QBI98-931

*To the women who cultivated the land
for the growth of their children*

Books by Linda K. Hubalek

Butter in the Well
Prärieblomman
Egg Gravy
Looking Back
Trail of Thread
Thimble of Soil
Stitch of Courage
Planting Dreams
Cultivating Hope
Harvesting Faith (1999)

Acknowledgments

Thanks to all the family members and Salemsborg neighbors who helped with *Cultivating Hope*. The invaluable help from some of the sixth generation of descendants, namely Bethany, Benjamin, Laura, and Jason Carlson gave me the perspective I needed to see the importance of this land for the younger generation. Thank you for showing me the reason our ancestors cultivated the Kansas prairie for us.

Tack så mycket.

Linda Katherine Johnson Hubalek

Table of Contents

Johnson Family Chart

Family from 1869-1886

Samuel Fredrik, born July 29, 1836
Christina Charlotta, born December 15, 1844
Married May 10, 1862

Children

1. *Carl Johan Oscar*, born January 22, 1864

2. *Emilia Christina*, born March 5, 1866

3. *Josefina Mathilda*, born December 12, 1868
   died 1870

4. *Axel Frithiop*, born March 18, 1870
   died 1870

5. *Luther Gilbert*, born December 28, 1873

6. *Theodore Emanuel*, born May 7, 1876
   died January 18, 1884

7. *Esther Josephina*, born Sept. 9, 1878

8. *Almeda Maria*, born October 2, 1880
   died January 19, 1884

9. *Joseph Nathanial*, born January 6, 1884

10. *Herbert Theophilus*, born October 8, 1886

Foreword

Can you imagine being isolated in the middle of a treeless grassland with only a dirt roof over your head? Having to feed your children with whatever wild plants or animals you could find on the prairie? Sweating to plow the sod, plant the seed, cultivate the crop—only to lose it all by a hailstorm right before you harvest it?

This second book in the *Planting Dreams* series portrays my great-great-grandmother, Charlotta Johnson, as she and her husband build a farmstead on the Kansas prairie. Each chapter features a glimpse into her homesteading years. A mixture of fact and fiction, these individual stories show how the seasonal weather of the Great Plains affected both the cycle of farming and Charlotta's growing family.

I wanted to answer so many questions as I researched my ancestor's family. What was it like to be the first to cultivate this patch of prairie? How did they survive those first years in the dugout? Who were their neighbors they helped and depended on? How did Charlotta handle not only the day-to-day life situations but the tragic events that occurred? What emotions did she experience when she lost four children? Death is part of the cycle of life, but did it affect her outlook on homesteading?

As I stand on her land, I can imagine the dreams Charlotta would have had for her acreage and her children, but it is difficult to comprehend all the work, frustrations, and setbacks she faced to make it a reality. Years of hard work developed the land and improved the quality of life for her family—but not without a price.

As a child, I remember seeing two photos in an old family album of a boy and a girl lying in their coffins. There were no names on the photos, but I was told they were the children of my great-great-grandparents. While I was working on this book, a cousin of mine found a large photo of these same two children lying side by side in their caskets. A short time later, he found a photo of the family standing in front of their house during winter, minus these same two children. The cardboard mounting on the two photos was almost identical, so I deduced that the photographer took both at the same time. My childhood curiosity about Charlotta's children was finally satisfied.

The farming spirit of my ancestors continues through our family today. Descendants still own their original eighty acres and other land in the Smoky Valley area. Charlotta and Samuel planted and cultivated dreams in their little patch of Kansas prairie, and their family reaped the benefits.

My connection to Kansas is strong because Charlotta planted her Swedish roots in the prairie. And I hope it will spread to you, my reader, as well.

L. K. H.

Summer

1869

Hoeing Sunburn

I dip my callused hands into the basin and splash water on my hot, swollen face. The bucket of water is warm, not the cold and refreshing sensation I long for. It is sitting on a bench beside the dugout door and has absorbed the day's heat. I feel both relief and a stab of pain. My skin is parched from sunburn and wind, and the water stings my face instead of cooling it.

The wind whirls up without warning and snatches my head scarf that I have just taken off. It whips through the air, caught in a whirlwind, circling up and down in the tiny funnel of air. I chase after the scarf as it hops and skips across the prairie before being snagged on a clump of grass. Wearily I retrieve the bit of cloth and wrap it around my head again. My callused fingers fumble with a knot that will hold against the wind.

I am blistered from head to toe. Every movement hurts, yet I have no choice but to keep going until my muscles harden or give out. My eyes sting from squinting in the sun and wind. My dainty traveling gloves wore out when we were digging the dugout. From the pain I think the blister on my right little toe has become cracked and bloody.

And I'm not done for the day. I just came in to check the children and get a drink of water. There is so much to do, and for the time being I'm the only one here to do it.

Because of the expense of building our farmstead, Samuel has taken a job. It is both a trade-off and a standstill because it is time away from the field work. Both jobs need to be done, but neither can be performed without the other. The farm will not produce the money we need until we plow and plant it. But we can't afford the equipment or seed until we have money available.

At least there is help nearby if I need it. Although our group that traveled together from Illinois is spread across the prairie, someone is always within walking distance. But it is hard to visit neighbors because I would have three small children in tow. I don't have a horse and wagon for transportation.

Members of our church group have banded together to provide help and share expenses. Rather than all the men leaving at once, neighbors have united as a team on both the farm and the railroad job. Two men leave home to labor while the third takes his turn working on his farm and watching over the other two families. None of us can afford oxen and equipment by ourselves, but together we can by sharing the cost and the time.

Now it's Samuel's turn to be gone. He is somewhere out in western Kansas building the railroad bed heading across America.

So, I'm here alone with three children to feed and an acreage that is fighting change. I can't seem to get much done besides taking care of the children, but time must be spent hoeing the garden and the field. We were late planting, and production isn't as far along as I had hoped, so I need to help the plants as much as I can. My main goal is to get the vegetables that are growing next to the dugout harvested, dried, and hung in burlap sacks from the dugout ceiling.

I'm impatient to see progress for our work and sweat. I can't expect much in only a few months' time, but I need to feel that I have accomplished something on this farm other than merely surviving. We have planted very little of our eighty acres except for the garden and a small patch of corn. Neighbors worked together to build shelters for everyone. This winter we'll have to survive on hunting and the vegetables I harvest from the garden. We don't have our own animals yet, so we don't have to worry about winter feed for livestock.

Some days I hate this land. I want it to change its ways for me, but instead it fights back. The prairie doesn't plan to be captured and tamed. I pray for rain but instead the sun bakes the ground I'm trying to nurture. When nature does send moisture, it has been in the form of thunderclouds that can bring high wind and hail.

I'm afraid that I'm stuck with it, no matter what the outcome or the hardship it brings. We can't afford to buy what we need to make life comfortable. Our lives have to be sustained by this land.

At times I yearn to go home. Life was tough in Sweden, but at least we had a roof over our heads, a cow to milk, and family near us. It doesn't bother me when I'm out working on the land, but it weighs on me at night when I'm tired and discouraged.

We were so optimistic our first week on this land because we could only improve our situation. I soon found out that nothing could be worse than arriving on the empty prairie with no shelter and limited supplies. Living in a tent grew tedious. The constant struggle wore us down. The relentless wind tested my spirit and tired the children. Before the dugout was done, I was ready to crawl in the uncompleted hole to hide from the wind and sun.

The grass where our home was to be built was clipped, then the ground cut into sod bricks and laid aside for the roof. It was difficult digging up the prairie sod. The roots fought the shovel and break plow because they had been growing for generations before we cut into it. But that made a good solid brick because in the early summer, the moist soil is thick with new roots. Samuel commented that sod bricks cut during the fall would have been dry, crumbly, and more apt to undermine the construction.

Once the hole was dug, sandstone gathered from the buttes were used to reinforce the walls. Next we hardened the sides and dirt floor with a mixture of water, clay, and salt. The men made trips to the river east of us to find trees for ridge poles and limbs for rafters. No one could spare sawed lumber for roof beams.

The sod bricks were laid around the perimeter to add more height to the walls, and a single layer was placed on top of our makeshift rafters of dried grass and branches. Samuel stood one tree trunk under the ridge pole in the middle of the room to support the weight of the roof. The position of the support is inconvenient, but I prefer that to having the sod cave in on us.

A vent pipe for a stove was installed when we laid the dugout roof. I hope to have a little cooking stove inside the dugout before the first cold blast hits the plains this winter. For now I prepare our meals outside in a rock-lined pit that I can only use when the wind is not blowing. So far this summer, we have had more cold meals that hot.

When it was my turn at the shovel, I complained about digging such a big hole, but now I wish we had made it larger. We didn't have many possessions to store, but they filled up the hole quickly when we added our makeshift furniture.

Our new home felt dark and close at first with only the single door and the small window pane on the west. I felt like a trapped animal because there was no way out if something should happen and the single entrance were blocked. Now, most days I feel secure in the dugout because it is away from the openness of the prairie sky.

The main thing I have had to get used to is the dirt. When it is hot and dry, dust covers food and bedding alike. When it rains, the roof leaks and everything is splattered with the dripping mud. No matter how much I try to keep my little home clean, it will never truly feel that way.

The major need on our farm now is water. I didn't realize how much of it our family used for drinking and washing until we didn't have a handy source. We took well water for granted in Sweden and Illinois. Now our water is hauled from a creek a quarter mile away. We have a barrel to store it inside by the door and another outside on the corner of our shelter that catches rainwater. The men are working together to dig a well for each homestead. Until it is our turn, I have to be patient for a convenient water supply.

It took awhile to become accustomed to the heat, not only the temperature but the humidity. We thought the weather would be the same as in Illinois, but it is different in Kansas. Here there are no rows of trees to slow down or buffer the force of the wind.

There is so much about the Great Plains and its inhabitants that we don't know. And the only way to learn is by living with it.

I pick up the hoe and head back to the garden. The prairie is threatening to overtake my work.

The tiny glow of the burning feather in the bowl of tallow makes an effort to shine past the edge of the table. Its shadow barely lights our belongings that clutter the walls and floor space of the dugout.

The makeshift table is but wooden grocery crates stacked together. Two cracker barrels are our only chairs. If both Samuel and I are present for a meal, the children stand to eat. Eventually Samuel plans to make more chairs, even if they are tree stumps cut down from the river bed.

More crates stacked four high with their open ends out line the north wall and serve as shelves. Every time we have purchased crackers or the like, I've kept the tin, just to have containers to hold our food staples. Flour and meal will be spoiled if left open to pests. Another box holds our plates, cups, and silverware, many of which Samuel carved out of wood. Baking utensils and pans take up another. Personal items, like the brush and comb, lie on top of the stack. I had our few books there until the first night's rain soaked the covers.

I hung my framed embroidery sampler of the Swedish table prayer at eye level on the wall to remind me of our Swedish past. A small strip of oilcloth is draped over the top of the frame to protect it.

The only other picture displayed is an illustration of a two-story house I cut out of a magazine and pasted on a piece of cardboard. It's my goal to some day be out of this dugout and into a home like the one pictured. To me, an American-style home is the image of success. A real farmhouse would mean that our hard work paid off on this homestead adventure. But at the rate we are going, I wonder how many years before I walk through its front door?

The wooden trunk that traveled with us from Sweden is against the east wall. Our winter clothes and extra bedding are folded in there along with anything we don't want to have investigated by the vermin that plague our underground home.

Whenever I look at it, our name and destination carved into the front of the trunk reminds me of our voyage. It is still hard to imagine the thousands of miles that it and our family have traveled in the past year and a half.

My wedding chest is wrapped in a gunny sack and tucked in a hole dug under the bed. It holds our money, important papers, and my jewelry. We can't risk having our savings stolen by thieves or losing our land documents in a prairie fire. It is hidden from sight by a layer of dirt and a board on top of it, but either one of us can get to it in a hurry if we need to, or leave it hidden if we have to flee.

Cloth bags of beans and dried fruit we brought with us from our Illinois farm hang from the corners of the ceiling. Two months from now I hope to have so much food hanging from the rafters that we have to duck our heads as we walk around the room.

Oscar sighs in his sleep. He is sprawled across his floor mat in front of the trunk. His arms are flung over his head and his feet reach almost past the bottom of the mat. He is growing so fast. I should have made the mattress larger to begin with.

The girls lie curled up facing each other on the big primitive bed that is perched against the south wall. Tonight they were so tired they sunk down into the prairie hay ticking without a word of protest. Emily's left leg twitches upward, then relaxes. I hope bedbugs and fleas don't wake them so we can have a good night's sleep. Josefina's thumb almost falls out of her mouth until by habit she sucks it back in.

Our meager summer clothing hangs on the wall when it isn't on our backs. I take my nightgown off the buffalo horn wedged between two wall stones and replace it with my dress that I just took off.

I dip the washcloth in a bowl of dingy water, wring out the excess, and wipe the sweat from my face and chest. Oh, how I long for a clean cool bath in a tub. I've used the same water to wash the children earlier, and it smells of dirt.

My skin itches when I rub across the mosquito and chigger bites that cover my body. Something is crawling up my neck. I wipe it off with the cloth and hold it up to the light. Another tick. I flick it into the hot flame and watch it sizzle.

Out of learned habit, I shake my grimy nightgown before pulling it over my head, and three miller moths flutter away from their hiding place.

I give a quick blow to snuff out the burning feather. It is pitch black for a few moments until my eyes adjust to the light that is coming through the little window. Two steps from the table, and I ease into bed beside the girls.

Sleep eludes me as I think of things I did and did not do today. I can't get the thoughts of work out of my head. It has been another exhausting day trying to make progress on our land. Tossing and turning just makes the narrow stone walls of the dugout close in tighter. I stare at the ceiling. Dirt falls down in the moonlight onto my uncovered feet. Now that the room is quiet from the family's activities, the rodents are busy overhead.

My eye catches the moonlit handle of the hoe that is leaning in the southwest corner. The hand tool is always standing by the door because I never leave the dugout without it. The worst terror I have had to face on the prairie so far is the snakes silently slithering in the grass. They are so thick that I've lost count of how many I have killed this summer. And after you kill one, you must be on the lookout for its mate. More than once I've found a rattlesnake sunning itself in front of the dugout, and I've had to hack it to death and toss it out of the way to get in the door.

The shovel beside it dug out this home and has turned over countless cuts of sod to expose native soil for the garden. After only two months the metal point is dull and needs to be sharpened again. The tools we had packed for the voyage and the few we accumulated in Illinois are also stashed there. Samuel hung the ax and the gun over the door to keep them out of the children's reach but still handy for us.

It has grown stuffy inside, and I need air. I crawl out of bed, pick up the hoe, and ease outside. I pause to leave the door open to hear the children, but then shut it behind me so no nocturnal creature slips in unnoticed.

Ah, relief flows through my thin cotton shift as the breeze touches my skin. Such a contrast. I'm hot and cramped for space inside the dugout, but outside there is no boundary.

The wet grass glistens in the moonlight. Earlier this evening we had a gentle rain that cooled the heat of the day. It came so softly that I smelled it before I heard it, and for a change it brought no wind with it. The rain may make high humidity tomorrow, but tonight it feels heavenly.

I lean against the hump of the dugout to stare at the night sky. Its dampness soaks through to my skin. I'd love to go for a stroll but don't dare take the chance. There aren't defined country roads like there were in Sweden or Illinois. The dugout blends in so well with the scenery that I could get lost in the dark. With no landmarks visible I couldn't rely on my sense of direction. The light would show through the dugout window if I lit it, but there would be danger leaving it lit with sleeping children inside. And what would happen to my little family if something happened to me?

I walk around the dugout twice, then settle back to watch the heavens. I rub my abdomen. I must take care of myself for another reason, too. My tiredness isn't being caused by the workload only. Samuel doesn't know it yet, but we'll have another mouth to feed this spring.

The last wisps of clouds pass the full moon and open the sky to a brilliant display of thousands of tiny lights. The night light is so bright that I can see my shadow. Except for the dark contrast in the southwestern buttes, I can turn every direction and not see an obstacle in the horizon. I long to see the black silhouette of a single tree, but it will be years before that wish is fulfilled on this land.

I can't help comparing the Kansas summer sky with Sweden's. My parents and I gaze at the same star constellations but in different skies. The moon rises here in the evening around eight o'clock during the summer. In my homeland the sun would stay up past midnight, giving the moon only a few hours in the sky.

My mind floods with memories when I think of the summer sky there. We always stayed up all night on Midsummer's Eve to celebrate the return of the sun. The swaying birch trees in the evening breeze shaded friends and family sitting on blankets below. I can taste the feast spread between them: boiled crayfish, rye bread, and the first cherries of the season. The air, scented with fragrant purple lilac blooms and evergreen boughs, is filled with laughter. We celebrated the sun in Sweden. Here I'm thankful when the moon rises instead because it means the end of the work day, the heat, and the loneliness.

I consider "what if" situations in my head, and they bounce between continents and lifestyles. I must remember the reason we left Sweden, but I also wonder what would have happened if we had stayed. Letters from our parents tell us that waves of people are still leaving the county, so we were some of the first to leave in '68.

What if conditions turned around in Sweden? Then there would be fewer people and more land, and maybe we could have stayed. Of course, there were other problems to consider. People are leaving because of taxes and the church as well as the famine.

Will it pay to be the first family to plow this patch of Kansas prairie? I smile when I think of the excitement of the first day on this land. To call eighty acres our own went to our heads. Oh, the euphoria to finally be at our destination and know we had our own place. We knew it would be work, but we had high ambition.

In some ways we were naive, because it is going to take more sweat and money than I imagined it would. The prairie has been here a long time, and it is resistant to change. Can we survive the five years it takes to prove up this claim?

The little sod we have tackled has been tough to plow and has re-rooted when given the chance. Corn seed planted has to share moisture with the grass growing around the tender stalk. The pumpkin vines weave among clumps of re-established blue-stem grass. It will take more than one year to turn the fields into mellow soil.

The prairie calls me back to the land. Crickets and locust vocalize their tunes with the toads. Fireflies blink on and off as they float in the darkness. Mosquitoes persistently buzz in my ears no matter how I try to swat them away. A prairie wolf calls to another in the far distance; together they echo back and forth. The grass is silent because it is heavy with rain. I hate to say it, but tonight I miss the wind.

I scan the sky to search the stars, but a movement from the north catches my eye. I can't figure out how close it is, but I imagine an animal is foraging for an evening meal. Several species look for food during the cooler evening hours.

I look back to the north and realize it is a human walking across the prairie. I crouch down beside the dugout so my lone figure doesn't show. Our home is so low to the ground that a person could walk right by it and not realize it is there.

Who would be traveling at night? Usually a person would stop to sleep unless he wanted to travel while the air is cooler—or to be unnoticed. I don't know if he is a kind soul lost on the prairie or a thief in the night.

I don't think it is an Indian. We've seen them travel along the creeks now and then. They haven't threatened anyone in our group but have learned to recognize our dugouts as sources of food. Settlers in other parts of the state have been attacked by Indians when they have resisted, so a few stolen biscuits is a sacrifice I'm willing to make.

I see the flat top and brim of a hat on the man. I hold my breath. I'm more scared of the Texas cowboy than I am of the native.

The man stops. The brim of the hat points up, apparently looking up to the stars to find his direction. Now he is changing the angle of his path. Can he smell the remnants of tonight's cook fire? Does bright moonlight betray our dugout's outline?

My chest is pounding so hard he can probably hear my heartbeat over the sound of the crickets. Should I go inside and barricade the door, hoping the traveler doesn't see our home?

This is the first time that Samuel and I have been apart during our seven-year marriage. During the second night alone, I had panicked after hearing sounds outside the dugout door. I've always had my father or husband to protect me. It terrified me when I realized I was in charge of guarding my family. I spent the rest of the night sitting up at the foot of the bed with the shotgun in my lap and my sleeping children behind me.

I peek over the dugout. There is something familiar about the rhythm of the stranger's walk, the way his shoulder slants as his carries his baggage. I know that gait and stature. It's Samuel! He must have traded off work with someone, taken the train back to Salina, and decided to walk home tonight.

"Samuel! Samuel!"

I wait for him to answer or at least turn this way, but he keeps walking. He is about fifty yards away and must not have heard my hoarse voice above the din of the prairie life.

Can he find our dugout by himself? He has made it this far, but I'd hate for him to walk past me. I consider crawling to the top of the dugout to stand up higher, but I'm not sure that the roof has settled enough to hold my weight. I'd hate to fall in on top of a sleeping child and then still have Samuel walk past our crushed family.

On an impulse I pull off my nightgown, wave it in the air, and yell again. Samuel stops to stare at the flash of white. He waves back with his hat. Now he knows the prairie location of his family and home.

Then I wait, wrapped in the prairie moonlight, for the arms of my husband.

1870

Burial Wind

The summer wind is already blowing at first light this morning. It will turn hot and blustery before noon. Today I don't feel like fighting it. I wish it would just blow me away.

A year has passed since my family stood on this northeastern corner of our land. We planted rye from our homeland on this very spot. Now there are just four of of us instead of five. At the time I had so much hope in my heart for this land. Now I just feel empty and miserable.

Chunk, chunk, chunk. I listen to the rhythm of the shovel as it is raised and dropped into the ground, over and over, making the little hole larger and deeper.

A vibrating thud echoes through my ears, and I wince in pain. "Oh God," I ask in prayerful thoughts, "help me through this day." I'm sure every time I use a shovel again and happen to hit an underground stone or piece of buried wood, I'll remember this moment.

The thud means that what we were looking for has been discovered. Samuel has found the coffin of our little daughter, Josefina.

Chunk, chunk, chunk. He continues to shovel soil from the hole, then throws it into an increasing mound beside the grave. Oscar asks a question, but I can't comprehend it in my pain. Emily has wrapped her arms around my waist. She turned her head into my side when her father hit the underground wood.

Samuel pauses as the thrust of his shovel continues to bring the sound to his ears. He questions me with stone-cold eyes but then continues clearing the soil again from the side of the box. He is digging another place for the coffin of another child. We have only been here twelve months, and the prairie has already claimed two lives.

I peer down into the hole. The wooden side of the pine box is damp, but it has not been in the ground long enough to start decaying. I can still envision her sleeping inside just as I placed her a few months ago.

Perhaps it seems odd, but I insisted that Samuel dig down beside the other grave because I wanted Axel's coffin to touch Josefina's. That way they would be together. That was the only way Samuel could find to console me. I imagine them holding hands together in their final sleep, just as the two had done briefly in life.

Although only fifteen months old, Josefina was captivated with her infant brother when he was born in March. He was a human being her size; she could get close to him and look into his eyes. Axel would stare back, fascinated with his toddling sister.

More than once when Axel was sleeping in the makeshift cradle, she would attempt to crawl in with him. I finally gave up trying to separate them for naps and put them together in our bed. The little girl always laid facing Axel, one arm wrapped around his little body. At first the baby fussed, but soon he wouldn't go to sleep without her. I had such a time with Axel after she died. His security was gone.

Josefina died before reaching her second birthday, and now Axel follows her before he had a chance to take his first step. Today they will be back together again. Two babies who never got the chance to explore the prairie. Now they will be a part of this piece of ground forever.

Axel, my fourth child, was the first baby conceived and born on this land. Pregnancies are a way of life, but I was apprehensive about giving birth in the dugout in the middle of nowhere. In both Sweden and Illinois doctors were available to help in an emergency. Here I had to depend on the help of Samuel and a neighbor.

We were happy with the event of the boy. Now there was another son to farm the land. But our hopes disappeared with the last rays of yesterday's sunset.

I'm not sure what they died from, but it was probably summer complaint. Josefina was a healthy child until the last few days of her life. She had a tummy ache, started diarrhea, then didn't last long after that. I'll never know for sure what caused her death, and we had no doctor or medicine to give her a chance at recovery. Little Axel went the same way.

I have prayed for the children's safety every time they have gone outdoors. Bareheaded and running barefoot, I worried that the elements and the prairie's natural dangers would harm them. Instead they died in the dark dugout, away from the sunshine and its beauty.

We would have liked to have had them buried in the new church graveyard, but that hasn't been plotted yet. I'm afraid there are many lost souls being buried in the prairie this year. They couldn't wait for our congregation's future plans. Now, no matter what happens in the future, I will always have ties to this land because of this corner burial ground.

The ground is hard, and Samuel sweats at his task. I know he would rather be doing this, digging, sweating, moving—anything to keep busy—than thinking about the loss of another child.

It didn't take him much time or wood to make the tiny boy's coffin. Lumber sells at a premium, and one hates to have to use it for such a purpose. But this is one of the reasons it is kept on hand.

The bottom of the hole is now level with that of the other box. Samuel stops his digging and crawls out of the grave. We stand immobile, forlornly looking down at the place we'll lay our next child. Oscar and Emily shouldn't have to see this twice, but they know that everything dies; the bird, the calf, and sometimes even a child. I shudder to think that one of them may be next. Sadly, there is no guarantee in life.

Samuel and Pastor Dahlsten lower the coffin into the ground and push one box solid against the other. I hear more of it than I see because of my blurred eyes. I know that I cannot change the cycle of life, but it hurts that two of my babies did not get the chance to live. Samuel and I have made sacrifices to make life better for our children, but they weren't enough for Josefina and Axel.

Each of us drops a handful of soil on the coffin to commit Axel's body to the earth. My mind flashes back to my mother slowly pouring her handful of soil on my baby sister's grave in Sweden. She did it a few grains at a time, trying to prolong the task as long as possible, because the next step was filling in the hole forever.

The pastor prays to God to take care of our son, then Samuel picks up the shovel and starts filling the hole. The loneliest sound in the world is the first shovelful of dirt thrown onto a coffin. I turn away before the simple wood boxes disappear under the weight of the earth.

How could God take away another child? Are we being punished for wanting a piece of His land? Were we selfish for wanting more than what we had in Sweden? Both these children were born in America. Why couldn't they survive in their native land?

I search the open sky for help, but it only answers back with the wind. A gust tries to sway me back and forth with the sea of grass, but I just lean into it the way I've learned to do this past year.

It can not blow me down because I am anchored to this land. I have sunk my roots into the prairie, and nothing can pull me away. The wind turns around to gently dry the tears streaming down my face and gives me the answer I needed to hear.

No, as much as it hurts, I realize I can't blame God or myself. Death is just a part of nature, and these two children were not meant to be stewards of this land.

1872

Hailing Dreams

Many times over the past three years I have climbed out of the dugout, walked to the highest point of our land and stepped inside my imaginary house. Like a child in play, I'd daydream about each room and its contents.

In my mind, the piping hot pie I pull out of the wood oven fills the air of the kitchen with the scent of apple and cinnamon. As I set it on the worktable to cool, a bit of flaky crust breaks off, and I pop it in my mouth. Mmmm, it melts on my tongue with just the right amount of butter. I pinch off another bit of crust just to be sure.

I walk across the spacious kitchen to the pantry. Shelves on both sides of the small room are stocked with a variety of dishes, cooking utensils, and canned goods. I load my arms with a stack of china dishes for our next meal.

I pad into the carpeted dining room and place a plate at each imaginary chair circling the long table covered with a crisp white linen cloth. Soon my whole family will sit down to a wonderful dinner, all made from the riches of my garden.

The chatter of my children drifts in on the easy breeze of summer through the open dining room window. The fragrant whiff of purple lilac follows as a child in play brushes past the full-bloomed bush planted at the corner of the house. Looking out the window through the shade trees, the new red barn dominates the farmyard and the children playing in its shadow. Chickens scatter as a fat goose honks his way through their flock. Contented cows graze in the belly-high meadow grass beyond the outbuildings.

The latest baby cries for me, and I glide into the side room to pick up the infant from his ornately carved cradle. The bedroom is simply furnished with a large bed that has both head- and footboards, a mirrored dresser topped with brush, comb, and jewelry box, and a wash stand holding a china chamber set.

Moving to the parlor, I sit down in our Victorian rocking chair to soothe the child back to sleep. The chair rocks silently on the colorful area carpet. A walnut settee and two chairs matching the rocker in design finish the conversation circle around me. A four-foot-high whatnot stand displays pretty glass dishes and bric-a-brac in the corner of the room. A parlor table, draped with a white embroidered runner, sits in front of the lace-framed window. A small group of family miniatures is displayed in front of the glass kerosene lamp. The clock ticks on the shelf that hangs above the book case. The smooth walls are covered with gold and blue wallpaper print.

The ceiling is . . . but now my eyes focus on clouds above me, and I pull out of the dream. For some reason the sky always brings me back to reality. I never get upstairs in my dream house; it is always the first floor only.

I could only visualize the day it would happen. At times I didn't have faith that we would make it. We had so many doubts and obstacles in our way that it was hard to see the progress we were making our first seasons.

Time has changed the prairie around us. There is still some land in the area that is yet unclaimed, but most of our section has been spoken for. Neighbors have started raising buildings, so rather than a continuous prairie the land is now dotted with cluster of homesteads. Within our sight, several families are moving above ground. We can see Lindholm's progress just to the east of us. His brother, Gust, is moving in south of us. Nystynd's farmstead now looms on our western horizon. The Applequists, Andersons, and Ecklunds are beyond our vision on the east.

It is good to see change in the landscape because it is a sign of progress, but in some ways I miss the unbroken rolling grass.

It was daunting at times, but it also was comforting once it became familiar. I learned the breath of freedom here.

The dugout made me feel I was a part of the prairie because I was living in it. But I also felt that it was holding me down, trying to keep me at its level. I'll miss the security I've learned to appreciate from our first home, but I won't miss the dirt and darkness.

After three years' work, we have plowed and planted enough acres to make a down payment on materials for a house. To me, starting this structure shows that we have survived and are making progress. Now that we're building above ground I feel that we're accomplishing a major step, be it one board at a time.

Evenings for the last year have been spent planning and dreaming about this little house.

Where shall we put it? The best place would be the highest spot on our land, where we can see out to all directions. We decided to build next to the dugout, then in the future as we add on to the house, we can use the dugout as part of the basement under the new section. We have already dug one hole in the ground, so it could be expanded in the future to the size we need. Once abandoned the dugout would eventually sink back into the earth. We might just as well use it as have to fill in the hole.

How big should we make our new home? Shall we use native stone or buy lumber? When discussing the house plans I imagined our house in Sweden but realized there are so many other possibilities because we're in America now. We will stay with a practical design because of cost but not because of Swedish tradition.

Our goal is to build a starter home now, just a simple rectangular wood-frame design, and add on in the future. My favorite house illustration still hangs in the dugout. It's been stained by water dripping from the dugout ceiling and it's covered with fly specks, but I'm keeping it for future reference. Someday we'll be able to afford the porch prominently shown in the picture.

Our house will consist of two rooms, one for cooking and living and the other for sleeping. The stove will be in the kitchen, placed against the middle wall of the house so the chimney will heat both rooms. A steep staircase on the north wall will lead to the unfinished attic that will be used for storage and extra sleeping quarters. Two windows will be set in the west side, with a door between them leading outside to the yard, another window in the south wall, and a door and window on the east.

How much will it cost? What can we afford? Samuel made a trip to Salina to find out the price of lumber, windows, doors, shingles, and all the hardware that goes with it. With so many families homesteading in the area, the lumberyards are busy with orders. Lumber was scarce and expensive three years ago, but now that Salina is connected to the world by rail, lumber is shipped in from a saw mill by the carloads at a more affordable price. To reduce time and waste, the house is sized so the twelve- and sixteen-foot-length boards don't have to be cut. The walls will be spaced on sixteen-inch centers to handle the forty-eight-inch lath sticks that will hold the plaster on the inside walls. Any tricks of the trade to save costs and time will be utilized.

Can we secure financing now to pay it off later? A visit to the banker procured a note against this year's harvest to make the first payment to the lumberyard. All we have to worry about is the weather between now and wheat harvest!

Who should we ask to help with the framing? The floor plan was simple enough that professional help was not needed, but extra hands were for the framing. This is where neighbors come in handy. But there was a lot of preparation involved before we were ready to call in assistance.

Beginning work was done this spring between planting, rains, and chores. First a trench was dug to define the size of the house. We won't have a basement under this part of the house. Rock and mortar would be the cheapest foundation rather than a cement base. It became a family project to head for the buttes in the early light and spend our mornings digging stone from the hills. A shovel, pick rod, and hands were our tools. With a wagon load by mid-morning, we would head back downhill. I'd prepare our dinner while Samuel and Oscar unloaded the stone.

After dinner, stone was picked out and stacked in place. A mortar mixture of lime, sand, and cement powder was worked in between the rocks to hold them solidly. The top layer of stone had to be hand-chiseled to make it flat and the right height.

A week before the planned framing, Samuel made several trips to town to get the supplies. It was fun to see what he brought home each time. We unloaded stacks of 2-by-4 lumber, rolls of tar paper, bundles of lath sticks, small kegs of square nails, horizontal siding, and bricks for the chimney. Some items were stored inside the dugout to keep them out of the weather. I didn't mind the intrusion as long as the crowded conditions meant I would soon have a real house.

I grew more excited as the lumber pile grew daily. The smell of fresh-cut lumber met me every time I came out of the dugout. I had been waiting three years for that smell.

Hammering, sawing, grunts, and shouts. The hill on our farm is a buzz of activity as the men work on the house frame this morning. I can't believe the day is finally here. Wagons loaded with men and their tools arrived before morning rose in the east. It was best to get part of the work done before the day grew hot. Sandberg, Applequist and Lindholm came together. The Thelander brothers arrived behind them. John Carlson and his son Carl walked over from the west. Carlson's wife just died this spring, and we thought it would help to include them in the day. Young Carl looks like he could use a good meal.

I think Samuel and I were more excited than the children. I can't begin to describe how important this house is to us. This is what we have been working toward since we made the decision to leave Sweden. To be sure, owning our own land was the main part of our dream, but to have an American house standing at the top of our land . . . I can't wait to write to our parents when it is done.

My morning has been spent running in and out of the dugout carrying pots, dishes, and food to feed the people who will be here for dinner. Some of the wide floor boards we'll use later in the house were set up on barrels this morning to form a long table on the north side the dugout. It is one of those hot days that makes me wish our young spindly trees were large enough to shade the company. At least next time we have a group here to eat, I can serve them at a real table with a roof over it instead of on boards out in the open.

When Samuel called for a forenoon break, I was prepared. Using the basin and bucket of water I had set on one end of the makeshift table, the men washed up, then sat down on chairs, barrels, or crates around it.

They talk of their progress, what is going on at each other's farms, and the weather. I listen as I pour steaming hot coffee into their cups. Except for church, I am rarely off the farm, so I am interested in the conversation. I look up to the sky as they talk about the dry spell we're having. The weather has cooperated this morning with today's project. As usual, it is getting hot, but so far we don't have more than a slight breeze. For today that's fine. I don't want a stiff wind blowing when I'm trying to serve a meal outside, and we don't want a heavy rain to spoil our work schedule.

I uncover the food I had set under dish towels to deter the flies that buzz around the table. Thick slices of pie are dished out onto the two plates Emily is holding out, then she bashfully carries them to the men at the far end of the table. The men politely thank her, and she skips back to me for the next plates. We could have passed them down the center of the table, but she's at the age where she likes to help, and she needs to learn.

By the time I've made one round filling everyone's cup with coffee, it's time to make a second trip. The men help themselves to the bread, butter, and jam set in the center. Oscar sits with the men today, beaming that he could be a part of the framing crew. Even though he is young, he is expected to help build this house.

After complimenting our lunch, they resume their work. This isn't the first house that this group has framed this year, so they know how to work together. Lumber is measured and cut, hammered together, and the first wall is raised into place. Three outside walls, one interior, and one roof to go.

Another wagon—this time full of women and children—pulls in beside the dugout. The families of the men working here today have come over for the noon meal. It's an occasion for the neighbors to get together. Elizabeth Sandberg picked up Sofia Applequist and her children. I imagine Maria Lindholm and her six girls will walk over from the next acreage shortly. Her two boys arrived a short time ago and are helping Oscar with the smaller tasks. I asked about Hannah and Christina, the Thelander sisters-in-law, but Louis said they wouldn't be coming over since they live further away.

In short time we have the food, quilts, and babies unloaded for our picnic. It is so good to have the neighbor women here. Most of the time we only have our children to talk to, so everyone seems to be talking at once.

"You brought mulberry pie, Maria? Where did you find those?", asks Elizabeth. "I went up and down the creek, but I didn't find any trees loaded this year like the last. Did you dry them plain, or add a little sweetener first?"

I try to draw Sofia into the conversation. Her two-year-old Anna died in May, right after she gave birth to Albert. It's been a hard spring for her, so I'm glad the Sandbergs thought to pick them up.

The older girls sit at the far end of the table, giggling about something. I almost trip over another child. We have more than a half dozen young ones underfoot.

"Emily, show the children your new kittens." I hope the distraction will keep the children occupied until the meal is ready. Little hands keep sneaking up from below the table to snitch a morsel.

Fried chicken, creamed peas and potatoes, rye bread, green beans, pies. The table is loaded with the produce from our gardens. Each woman made something special for the occasion of visiting another farm. The men will enjoy our food, but we women relish the company.

A rumble. What? Was that thunder? Which direction did that come from? I shade my eyes with a soapy hand to scan the sky. We're clearing up from dinner. I have two more pots to wash in the wash basin sitting on our plank table, then we'll be through with dinner's dishes. Everything is spread out to dry. Maria and Elizabeth are drying the dishes while Sofia tends the babies. Some are contently sleeping under the shade of the table. The three little girls are making mud pies in the dirt, and some of the other children are playing with our kittens again.

A gigantic thunderhead is mushrooming in the west. It is building so fast, I can see it happening. It's high up in the ceiling of the sky instead of low. White cotton is puffing out as the front pushes toward us. If it keeps building, we could be in for a bad storm.

We need the rain, but not when it comes with potential damage. The men pause their work when the second rumble is heard above their noise. Samuel glances uneasily at the lumber, then at the men surrounding him. I can see by his look that he is wondering the same things I am. How far away is the storm? Are we going to be in its path? How much time before it hits the farm?

The lumber for the third wall is laid out on the ground, ready to be nailed together. Whack, whack, rings the hammers, in rhythm, then off balance as the men pick up speed. Should we stop and move the supplies in the dugout? Can the families make it home before the storm, or should they stay close by to seek shelter in the dugout in case it grows worse?

The sky darkens as the gray clouds descend and the storm rolls over us. Rain starts to fall, slowly, one drop here, one there, plunk, plunk, heavy with moisture, then faster. Before we have time to react, the wind sharply hits the two new standing walls, testing the temporary braces. Emily cries out as an empty tin plate becomes airborne and hits her in the head.

The men dash around the piles of lumber, grabbing tools to protect against their shirts that are now becoming saturated from the downpour. The cold front hits the farm as we herd the children into the dugout. Instantly the rain changes to slush, then tiny hail.

Everyone crowds around the furniture in the dugout as the yard fills with a layer of hail. Outside one of the mother hens dashes for cover, leaving the chicks trailing behind. One by one they are hit by the ice and tossed into the mud by the wind. There goes our egg money for the summer and our fryers for this fall.

"Hey, Charlotta," Carl Lindholm calls out to me, "do you have any milk and sugar? We could make a huge batch of ice cream with all this free ice!" I try to smile at his remark. I know he is trying to break the tension. Everyone is worried about their own farms as the storm surrounds the dugout.

I watch out the window as the storm hits the farm. Crack! A bolt of lightning hits nearby. The flash happened the same time as the sound. Did it hit a building or start a prairie fire?

I wonder about the dog but realize he was already in the dugout when we started cramming in. He can sense the bad storm before we can see it. The children carried the four kittens in with them, but I don't know where the momma cat is hiding.

I wish I would have had time to tip the wash tub over a tomato plant. By the looks of things, the garden is being destroyed.

The skeleton of my house leans against the force of the wind. The size of the hail increases to marble size. The sky has turned pitch black from the storm. The wind whistles as it tosses lumber in the air. Has the storm brewed a cyclone or just a very strong wind?

What about the crops? We're counting on the spring wheat harvest to pay the note on the lumber. It would have been cut next month. What will happen if we get hailed out? Can we get an extension on our loan?

I'm on the verge of tears. Why can't we get ahead? Why must the weather always threaten our hopes and goals?

1874

Invading Clouds

Sweat drips off my nose as I lean over to pull at a weed my hoe didn't dislodge. When the tool fails, I get impatient and revert to grabbing the reluctant plant with both hands for the tug-of-war. The roots do not want to let go of their anchor in the hard ground, and I end up with just the top of the plant in my green-stained hands as it snaps off at the base. Odds are it will grow back before the next time I go through this patch of the garden. Why do plants I'm trying to kill survive, and the ones I'm trying to nurture do not?

Long rows running east and west grace our land on the south side of the house. Looking from the distance I see hues of green tinged with yellow. Waves of heat rise and ripple above the fields. Up close the scorching effects of this July weather are apparent in the patches of squash, turnips, cucumbers, beans, and tomatoes. Leaves made ragged from this summer's hoppers give the garden a battle-scared look. A chicken darts past me at the sight of yet another such insect hopping between the plants. I've been dusting the garden with wood ash to deter them but have had only limited success.

The vegetable garden is surviving because we have carried water to sections of it. But heat alone can curb production if it is too hot for the budding flower that produces the fruit. We try to water everything but wonder which vegetable should receive the most attention. Which will give us the best return for the effort?

What will push itself beyond the stress of the drought if we give it the boost of an extra bucket of water?

Fuzzy pumpkin leaves sit limply along the vine's length. They are partially wilted not only from the afternoon sun but also because of the lack of rain. A few pumpkins have formed along the stretch of stems, but there are also shrunken balls that died before they had a chance to start expanding.

The bean vines aggressively climbed their tepee support this spring, but now brown leaves crackle and disintegrate when we reach among the vines for the pods. Some years the children could hide under the cool canopy and not be seen, but this month I've had to tie a sheet between two tepees to give shade to the sleeping baby cradled in the basket below. Gilbert's wisp of hair is stuck to his sweaty forehead even though he is only wearing a cloth on his bottom. There is no breeze this afternoon to dry his tender skin. Heat rash has plagued the poor infant all summer.

The potato tops have had a double jolt from the drought and the work of the potato bugs. Emily's frame is bent over the rows again, concentrating on her afternoon job. She has spent hours collecting insects from the plants, but their numbers and damage have taken their toll. Emily took it as a personal failure at her job when the tops dug up this week revealed small tubers. She has been picking off the bugs and carrying water to the plants, so why aren't the potatoes big and ready for harvest by now? How can I explain to an eight-year-old that the heat and stress of the drought are more powerful than her efforts or prayers?

I keep waiting for a good soaking rain that could change the garden. We've seen it before. If clouds build heavy with moisture—without mushrooming into a thunderstorm—we can get a decent inch of rain in an afternoon or evening. The transformation is incredible. Rainwater can turn everything a lush green overnight. But this summer the hot drying wind has whisked away any moisture before the plants have had a chance to claim it.

Will I be able to fill the cellar with produce this fall, or will the shelves have empty spaces? I asked Samuel to make more wooden bins for the root crops, but he hasn't gotten around to it. I don't know if it is because of his lack of time and materials or his lack of faith that the garden will produce the need for extra storage.

Oscar trudges by on his way to the orchard, trying not to spill any water from the full buckets he is carrying in his outstretched hands. He knows his countless trips back and forth between the well and the orchard will be rewarded eventually but right now he's puffing from the effort, red in the face, and grumbling about the task. The ground around the young fruit trees soaks up the water so quickly that it doesn't run off. The trees were planted three years ago, and this year we had a few sparse blossoms on the short twigs of the largest ones. My son is not carrying water to the trees to make these few fruits survive but to ensure the future of the trees themselves. Maybe there will be enough fruit for a pie or two next year. I hope this orchard lasts beyond my pie-making years. Right now the trees are no more than spindly sticks, as tall as Samuel, but they don't cast as wide as a shadow as he. In ten years I would like to see the whole east side of the farm sprinkled with blossoms in the spring, shaded with leaves in the summer, and heavy with fruit in the fall.

The pounding of Samuel's hammer echoes across the valley as he works on the siding of our barn. It almost sounds like someone is pounding back. It is such a still day that I'm sure the neighbors can hear it. We had help raising the skeleton of the building, but Samuel has been doing the rest himself whenever he has time. For months we could see through the building because the spring field work came first. Now in the lull of summer, he is working on getting the building enclosed before he starts on the harvest. Although not as big or as fancy as he would like, it will hold the horse team, milk cows, and a few other head of livestock. A hay mow overhead will protect a supply of dry hay.

Until now, the primitive lean-to was the animal's shelter. Covered with prairie grass, it has served its purpose longer than we had planned.

Right now the animals are picketed in the native grass patch west of the barn. Before dinner the animals were herded out by Oscar to graze. During the growing season the neighborhood children drive the animals together to the grassy buttes to the southwest of us. Now the cows lie in the grass, eyes closed, chewing their cuds as they digest the morning's food. The two draft horses stand side by side but face opposite ways so each other's tail can twitch at the ever-present flies. The only animals that seem to be active in this heat are the two calves. A minute ago I couldn't see them because they were curled up in the grass. Now they are springing through the meadow like children playing tag, occasionally bawling much like a youngster would scream for the delight of hearing it.

This summer has been one of our worst yet of the five we've worked on this land. We're needing rain badly to get any kind of yield from our fields. Every time we wake up to a cloudy morning, or see a red sunset, we hope that it will mean our drought will turn around in the next twenty-four hours.

The corn leaves are a green-gray, tinged with brown instead of a lush green. This time of year people claim to see the stalks growing overnight, but they are stunted this season. I worry that the plants won't have the energy to produce any ears. The broom corn should be stretching past the field corn by now, but there isn't much difference between them yet. The hay crop was thin and coarse.

The July sun bakes my back that is turned away from the western horizon. The slight summer breeze that made the afternoon bearable has disappeared, and I sense a change in the sky. I was concentrating on my task until I felt the wind shift.

My shadow disappears as a cloud covers the sun momentarily. Finally, a relief from the heat and maybe a change of weather. Looking to the west to search for rain clouds, I see a block of darkness coming over the hills, but it doesn't look like a normal, gray cloud. Could it be dust whirling in the air? The weather hasn't changed so that it feels like a cyclone. As the cloud comes closer, it changes back and forth from bright to dark specks as the sun shines on it. It almost looks like a snowstorm approaching.

Ouch. Drops pelt me from above, but it's not rain. Greenish-blue insects are falling from the sky. A few, then a constant barrage. What in the world? The ground is suddenly covered with one-inch-long grasshoppers. The sky has turned into a swirl of humming insects, dropping, hopping, clinging to everything. Not just a few hundred but thousands spreading so far west that I can't see the end of the gray intrusion.

Everywhere the ground is moving, crawling, jumping as the grasshoppers jockey for a position on the vegetation of the garden. I stand frozen, dizzy from watching the earth move. The noise level rises as the grasshoppers attack, their jaws devouring any bit of foliage in sight.

Gilbert starts to fuss, then shrieks in fright as the insects crawl over him. Running to his rescue, I grab him with one hand and dangle him in the air, scraping off the bugs with the other. Oscar and Emily yell and dance around, batting off the attackers as they run for the house.

As I scramble for protection, I see Samuel out in the meadow trying to pull up the rope stakes of the picketed horses to move them into the barn. They fight, rear, plunge at the attack of the insect cloud and its noise. The horses are trying to flee the bombardment and can't understand that Samuel is trying to lead them to shelter. They break free of Samuel's grasp and run away from the invaders, ropes and stakes dragging behind them.

We are still not away from the grasshoppers once inside the kitchen. I had the windows open, and they are crawling over the windowsills in droves. The mosquito netting we used to screen the opening from insects must have been devoured. We hastily close the windows but still have to take care of the hundreds already inside the house. They are jumping on and off the walls, the curtains, the table, and the stove. Anything they consider edible is attacked.

I rush into the bedroom with Gilbert and find the same scenario. The grasshoppers are clinging to the bedding and the clothes hanging in our bedroom. They are eating holes in the material right before my eyes. I have to shake out the sheet in the cradle before I can lay Gilbert down and throw it back over him. The insects move back onto the cloth and start eating again.

Grabbing the broom in the kitchen, I begin a sweep and swat motion, trying to kill as many at once as I can. But what to do with them next? I can't open the door to sweep them out for fear we will have just as many new grasshoppers invade the house.

Oscar is stepping barefoot on them, but that is more than Emily can manage. She wildly swings a towel at them, trying to keep them off herself.

Samuel slams through the back door, covered with more insects to kill. He chased the horses through the orchard and finally gave up to seek shelter for himself. His shirt has holes where the grasshoppers have eaten through to his scratched skin.

Samuel's face crumbles as he looks out the window and views the impact of the disaster. I had been fighting off the invasion and hadn't thought about anything else until I saw my husband's reaction. In shock I stop to stare out the window.

From the east window I can see the fruit trees are stripped of their fruit and leaves, and fresh exposed wood shines in patches along the trunks. Grass below the tree trunks has been eaten off to the roots.

The brown earth is just as smooth as before we planted the garden last spring. Every bit of vegetation in the garden is gone. There is now flat ground where the squash leaves rose before. The bean tepees are bare of any vines and are threatening to topple over from the weight of the crawling grasshoppers.

Only an occasional stump still stands in the field south of the house. The whole corn field has been leveled by tiny insects in just a scant amount of time.

There will be nothing to harvest this fall. It is all gone.

The main cloud of grasshoppers moved on by the end of that day, but we still had to contend with drifts of them against the buildings. Part of our daily task these last two weeks has been raking the insects into piles, dumping bushel baskets of them them into the yard, and burning their bodies into charred remains.

Everything inside the house is stained brown from their juice. Even after days of cleaning, I still feel sick from the smell of squashed bugs.

The mended curtains remind me of the ordeal every time I look out the windows. The invaders are still being found whenever we use an item: inside the butter churn we use once a week, between tins in the cupboard, behind picture frames on the wall, squeezed between the covers and spines of books, in pockets of winter coats.

And today tiny reminders hatched from the eggs laid in the cracks of the floor boards during the initial siege. I look forward to winter just because it means I won't have little grasshoppers gnawing on my bed sheets.

New grass has not had a chance to start growing again because there are still enough hoppers around to eat anything that tries to push out of the ground. And we have had no rain to help boost the vegetation's chances.

The animals that stampeded during the attack were found miles from home, but there was little for them to eat once they were brought back to our homestead. The first stacks of hay that had been cut and piled for winter consumption in June were attacked by the insects, leaving us short of fodder. The cows and horses have had to forage the few corn stalks left in the cornfield or hunt for grass still in the buttes.

My worry is how we are going to feed our family during the winter months ahead with the garden stripped. There is some food in the cellar but not enough to last until next year's harvest. We came to Kansas with nothing but the bare necessities, but at least we had the prairie and its bounty.

People from the Salemsborg congregation helped each other to build our homesteads, but this time there is no one to lend the neighboring hand. We are all in the same dire situation.

The harvest from the past two years had been low due to the dry weather, but we didn't expect such a catastrophe as this. I blink back tears when I think how much we have done with these eighty acres in the past five years and how quickly we were set back. At this rate we'll never prove up on our claim if nature keeps knocking us down every summer.

We did not leave Sweden to end up starving in another country. We've got to find a way to survive until next summer.

Fall

1874

Optimistic Harvest

It smells of newness. I love the rosin smell of fresh pine lumber. It's not quite the same as the forest scent in Sweden but hints just enough to draw me back to the towering pines that shadowed the countryside. The mental picture of green is comforting after the bare brown year we've had.

The heat from the wood stove thaws my face. It must have been lit hours ago for the building to be this warm. It was a chilly two-mile ride from home, and we were all bundled up to ward off the November wind. I unwrap the blanket that hides Gilbert's face, and he blinks at the brightness. My goodness, for a change we won't have to wear our coats to keep warm during the service!

Before hanging my cloak on a peg along the back wall, I touch a hesitant finger to the plaster to make sure it is dry. The smell of fresh paint lingers.

The four tall windows along the two long sides of the white sanctuary shine bright. It is almost blinding compared to the low light we were used to in the dugout church. A simple chandelier hangs from the ceiling, and lamp holders are centered between the windows. I can't wait to see the illumination it will give during an evening meeting.

I gaze at the front of our new church. The pulpit and altar we used in our old church have been cleaned and set in place. Most of the old bench pews also were moved, with new additions filling the larger space.

Reverently we walk down the aisle, surprised to hear the sound of leather soles against a wooden floor. Before it was the muffle and squish of shoes mired in mud between the pews placed on the earthen dugout floor. Sometimes it was so sticky the congregation would have problems leaving after the service. Our shoes were glued in place while sitting during a long sermon. Now we'll have to remember to clean our shoes before coming into the church instead of after leaving it.

Samuel counts each pew on our walk down the aisle, trying to decide where we should sit. From habit, he will choose from the right side of the church, about a third of the way up from the back. Our family's pew box in Sweden was on the right, and we automatically sat on this same side at the church in Andover and in the dugout. Most families gravitate to the same pew each Sunday, so we will claim the pew now that we'll sit in for the rest of our lives, or that of this church structure. Of course there will be times when we're late and visitors may have claimed our pew. But it is comforting to know that we have a permanent place in our new church.

Samuel stops, takes Gilbert from my arms, and motions me to the pew he has selected. Emily and Oscar follow me, then Samuel sits on the end. I think he took the baby so he could look back to see who is coming into the nave.

Neighbors file in, looking around, exclaiming over the new structure. I lean over the children and whisper to Samuel that the family that usually sits in front of us in the dugout will probably do the same here. He just smiles, knowing I am right.

Sister Hedda and her family slide in behind us. She married the widower John Carlson a year ago last spring, took in his eight-year-old son, and now has her own baby boy. I coo at the infant and put my hands out. Little Axel gives me a big smile and does not protest when Hedda hands him over the pew. My eyes mist a bit thinking how much he looks like my own Axel who died at this age four years ago. I hug the child and give him a quick kiss on the top of the head. I pray we get to see this child grow up. He was baptized in the sod church. I glance around the sanctuary, wondering which pregnant woman will deliver the first child to be baptized in our new church.

Salemsborg, the name chosen for our Lutheran church, was picked from a hymn out of the Swedish psalmbook. It told of a mountain where one could find peace at the end of life. When the name was picked, all involved in the organizational meeting hoped that this valley below the Smoky Hill Buttes would be our final home that we had traveled half the world to find.

Actually, two congregations were formed out of our Galesburg Land Company, one at each end of the buttes. Until last year, Pastor Dahlsten, who helped with our move to Kansas, served both churches. He traveled each Sunday for three years between the Freemount Lutheran Church and ours. One church would have service in the morning, then Pastor Dahlsten would ride to the other for the afternoon service, switching the times the following Sunday. Freemount has its own pastor now, and Pastor Dahlsten takes care of us.

In the past, we met in that old dugout. It was one of the first structures we built as a community. The men cut sod, hauled sandstone from the buttes, and carried roof lumber from Salina to fashion a crude enclosure that served our congregation for five years. It was important to have a place to gather together for worship, to provide strength and hope.

The building had problems in the beginning. The south sod wall collapsed from a heavy rain and had to be rebuilt before we could hold our first service. In addition to the muddy floor, we had to contend with God's creatures seeking refuge. Snakes had to be cleared from the building before each gathering. We held our first service there in November 1869. Now, five years later, our new building is completed, and today we are gathered for its first service.

The first families that settled here have grown in size. That's one of the main reasons we needed a new church and could afford to build one. Where there used to be a couple with a baby in the mother's lap there now sit two more children with them. At the same time, people continue to move into the church's district. We have more than six hundred members now. Rarely does everyone make it to church together because of the weather during certain seasons, but the old church was almost always full.

It took a miracle to finish the new building after the disastrous year we've had, but pledges had been made and the construction started. The loss of crop and livelihood because of the drought and grasshoppers tested our strength and pocketbooks as we continued building. Today we gather for a Thanksgiving service, to thank God that we have endured the year.

It has been a constant struggle since we were invaded by the grasshoppers this summer. I haven't experienced this feeling of doom since before we left Sweden. I still worry about how we are going to feed the children this winter. Donations, in the form of barrels of dried beans and clothing, have filtered in from concerned citizens from the East. We are already tired of eating beans at practically every meal, but we must be glad to have that. I keep reminding the children that there were people in other Kansas counties who suffered more than we have.

The weather has been dry all fall. There were no fall crops to harvest. The meager oats and wheat fields were threshed before the invasion, but we had low yields because of the drought. We cut and dried what grass was available. We want to keep our milk cows as long as we can. People have combed the creek and river banks gathering leaves for livestock feed. Others have sold their animals or butchered their stock.

We dug up the garden twice to make sure every tuber in the ground was found. This is not the fall to leave any produce unturned. A person watching us would have thought we had found gold because of the way we acted when a potato was unearthed.

The current weather makes me wonder if the drought will continue into next year or change its cycle. So far we are having a dry, cold spell with no snow. That could change without a day's notice and bury us in deep snow. At this point, we would welcome the moisture.

Samuel is thinking about finding an outside job for this winter. The rail track has been built to Denver, but there still may be work at Brookville's railroad headquarters. I'm against being left alone on the farm again, but we will do what must be done to feed the family and keep our land.

Voices of all pitches start the opening hymn. Some are strong, singing out each word with confidence, others are barely a whisper coming out of their throats. Each shows emotion in his own way—that person's personality and conviction. I can tell some people have left their troubles at the door to celebrate the new church and worship God, while others have carried them inside on their shoulders. I'm afraid I'm one of the latter as I muse about our farm's failure this year.

I glance from the page of the hymnal to the light beyond the windows. It seems to be darkening outside. Did a flake of snow just drift by the window? I look back to sing the next phrase, then my eyes dart back out. A flurry of snow is whirling about outside. Other people notice the change in weather, and the union of our voices falters.

Is it a dry or wet snow? Will we see just a few quick flakes, or is this a blizzard? How much will accumulate? Will it cause problems getting home or just brighten our ride? There are people here who traveled ten or more miles to be in church today.

I respond automatically through the service, but during the sermon my eyes and mind switch back to the weather. The pastor is probably thinking that in the old dugout his congregation didn't have the distraction of our large new church windows. Pastor Dahlsten's voice rises a notch to reclaim the attention of his followers. God's scene of nature outside is interfering with his sermon inside. But I see that the pastor's eyes also steal a few glances out the window. We are all excited about the prospect of moisture for our valley.

"Amen," says the pastor with bowed head. I mentally return to the service as the congregation rises for the end of the sermon. I have been sitting so long my knees are stiff. I hadn't noticed that Emily had fallen asleep while leaning against my shoulder, and she slumps over onto the bench as I stand up. One sleepy look up at her father and she rises to her feet. She is old enough to participate in the service and knows she better do just that.

People bundle up, leaving the church in a gay mood. Because of this service—and maybe with help from the outside scene, the dark cloud that has been hanging over our valley has been lifted for a while. There is a hint of hope for the future.

Light snow drifts down on our heads as we mingle with our neighbors outside the church. No matter the weather, this is our time to connect with the people who live outside the boundaries of our farm.

I peek under a blanket at a new baby in his mother's arms and am met with a wide-eyed stare. Oscar just charged around the corner of the church in pursuit of a game of tag. Emily is lugging around her eleven-month-old brother who is screaming to get down. Gilbert has had enough confinement during the service and wants to be free.

Samuel stands in a cluster of men who usually discuss the meager crop they have all had, almost trying to outdo each other with stories of worst situations. But today for a change they are talking with optimism about next year. Did the hope come from the passage of time, the new church, the snowflakes, or the camaraderie of other farmers?

I look around at the crowd milling about the steps of the church. All week we are isolated on our land, absorbed in the process of surviving and improving our piece of prairie. But on Sunday we gather, no matter how far away from this building, just to have human contact with other souls who are trying to do the same. It isn't just the word of God that nourishes our souls but also the connection with others who have the same background and goals we do. We receive comfort from our pastor and the Swedish hymns, but it is at this church gathering of people that we restore our faith in families and farming.

It will be a tough winter for everyone, but together we will survive another season on the prairie and look forward to another harvest, just because we are optimistic farmers.

1876

School Mud

Oscar balks going out the front door. "But there is still more harvesting to do! I can't go to school yet!" Yes, harvest comes first, but the weather prevents any work being done in the fields today. He knows that the wagons won't be able to get in the field after last night's heavy rain.

Emily shifts her pile of books from one hip to the other. She has her coat on and would have been out the door five minutes ago if she would have gone by herself. She meets the Lindholm girls at the end of their lane to walk with them. I suggested she and Oscar walk to school together today, and the request hasn't been well received by either child.

"Are you coming or what?!" Emily impatiently asks her brother. She's getting mad that she is missing out on this morning's play before classes. She has already been in school two weeks, and Oscar needs to get caught up. The children in the neighborhood attend the Sunny Corner Schoolhouse that was built four years ago.

The term is only three months long so Oscar needs to get started. Other boys will be starting school late too, so he won't be the only one. At twelve, Oscar thinks he is old enough to quit school, but I want him to continue his education as long he can. It's been hard to convince the boy that schooling is important when all he wants to do is follow in his father's footsteps. But learning to read and count will help him manage his own farm someday.

Samuel's father was a landholder and church warden who passed on to his sons his limited ability to scratch and cipher. I wasn't given the chance to learn much beyond church catechism. My parents were poor tenants who couldn't afford to send their children to school or hire a tutor. I'd say that Emily can read better than I.

Now we have a school nearby that can teach our children so much more than Samuel or I ever could, and we want them to take advantage of this opportunity.

"Now get out the door or you'll be late!" I retort to his outburst as I hand him his dinner pail.

Oscar takes off in a mad huff, with Emily in hot pursuit trying to catch up with him. Instead of walking down the lane to the road, they run around the house, cut through the orchard, zigzag down the muddy rows of harvested broom corn stubble, then run east parallel with the rough wagon wheel ruts that run in front of our farm.

I walk down our lane to the road to follow their journey. I stand on the road's edge, settle baby Teddy on my hip, and watch the two dash away from home. The orange morning sun is half risen on the horizon and gives a glow to the two figures running into it. I see a clod of mud fly high in the air as Oscar kicks the trail with his foot. Their shoes are now caked in mud from the path he chose.

So much for heading to school in clean clothes. I imagine there is mud clinging to the bottom of his trousers and her dress hem after taking their shortcut. Their clothes are also going to be soggy from the rain still clinging to the vegetation. Oh well, I doubt they will be the only ones in school with mud on their shoes and clothing. That's just the nature of children.

The prairie grass swings back into place after being parted by the children's strides. Raised voices drift back to the farm as their tall, skinny frames head over the hill. I don't think they realize that I, and our neighbors the Lindholms, can hear them arguing. It slowly fades as they move out of my hearing range.

The air is cool, wet, and heavy this morning. We farmers never complain about moisture—except when we are trying to finish a harvest. By the looks of the water standing between the corn rows, I imagine Oscar will be in school all of this week.

I pause to look north onto the open prairie. Not yet claimed or plowed, its grass towers above the floor of the plains. I missed the fall color of trees our first years here but learned to appreciate the hues that the prairie took on with the change of weather. While the big bluestem turns dark maroon, other grasses from switch grass to grama turn bright orange and rust to blend in with the ground color scheme. Texture varies from the tan seeds on the timothy grass heads to the fuzzy fox tails filling in as a mat below the taller plants.

Other plants add unexpected swaying patches of color. Milkweed pods have shed their white silk to spread their seed, then opened wide to show the prettiest pearl gold interior with a light pink tinge. Prickly bull thistle leaves protect anyone from coming close to the flower pods that are shedding their seed. Ruby red pasture rose hips scatter among a soft silver patch of sage. Dark brown centers of the black-eyed susan flower mix with faded flat tops of yarrow. Their white flower petals are long gone, but the smell still lingers when you crush the dried flower.

The prairie evolves each season from delicate pink rose petals and soft grass heads to bold yellow sunflowers of summer, then to the brittle seed pods of fall that I am viewing now. Winter snow and wind break down the plants to deposit the seed in the soil so the cycle can start again next spring.

A different set of weeds and wildflowers is anchored against the edge of our cultivated field. Plowing the native prairie has changed the landscape and allowed a new set of plants to prosper in the disturbed land. Stiff dark brown spears of curly dock contrast with the cream-colored fuzzy tops of goldenrod. From experience I know the pigweed plants will become tumble weeds traveling down the road, spreading seeds this winter as they roll across the earth.

Except for the native grass we kept for pasture and hay, the rest of our eighty acres has been plowed for field crops. Samuel and I have talked about buying more land, but it is beyond our means at this point in time. This farm isn't big enough to divide among three sons if they all choose to farm for a living.

We haven't finished the claim on this farm yet. Taxes are not due until the claim file is done, so we have been stalling with the final paperwork.

Land is still available in the area. All the homestead has been claimed, but the railroad still has land for sale. Not all is suitable for plowing, through. Some of the land around the buttes will never be turned because of the poor, rocky soil it features.

I hear the children. Did the winds shift so I can hear their voices again? Oscar is tearing back down the road toward me. Gilbert is tossed over his shoulder, kicking and screaming at the top of his lungs. He must have quietly sneaked out the east door to follow his older siblings. They weren't gone five minutes before one of them must have heard or seen Gilbert trailing behind. My guess is that a game of dodge and tackle had to be played before Oscar could catch Gilbert for the trip home. Gilbert is not quite three but always wants to be wherever his older brother is.

Oscar drops Gilbert at my feet, pausing for air and hoping that I'll change my mind about him attending school today. I point down the road, and Oscar lopes back down the trail for the two-mile trip to the school house. The ringing of the school bell can be faintly heard in the distance. Now he'll be late for his first day back to school.

1878

Shucking Weather

We have perfect fall weather today. The air is crisp with a tint of coolness in it and no clouds to block the afternoon sunshine. It is warm enough that we don't need coats, but not hot enough to sweat. No matter how far I look, there is a bright blue sky above. We couldn't ask for better harvest weather in October.

It was such a beautiful day I couldn't stay inside. Instead of sending Emily out with the afternoon coffee for the harvesters, she stayed in the house with Teddy and Esther, and I am going instead. Of course Gilbert is tagging along with me. We weave in and out of the harvested corn rows, listening for the sound of my men at work.

Thump, bang, swish. I can tell by the sound on the bang board of the wagon whose throw is whose. Everyone has his own rhythmic motion when he shucks corn. The wagon creaks as the horses pull up another few feet and stop. The team is trained to stay parallel to the row of corn being harvested. On Samuel's verbal command, they move to stay in line as the workers twist the corn off the plant, then throw it into the wagon beside them.

As we get closer, I see Samuel and Oscar through the stalks. Both heads are bent over, concentrating on their work. They don't look up at the wagon when they throw. By the time one hand tosses the ear of corn, the other hand has moved on to grab the one on the next stalk.

Oscar's growth spurt this fall has made him almost as tall as Samuel, although there is probably a fifty-pound difference between their frames. I imagine our son will tower over his tall father before he is through growing. I get a glimpse of Oscar's profile as he turns our direction. My oldest son is fair, and his face is sunburned beneath the protection of his brimmed hat. During the winter his red cheeks will fade to match his white forehead, but right now it is a striking contrast. He gets his fair skin coloring from me. Samuel is dark but also has a beard to protect his face.

The corn leaves rustle as we stride between the plants. I hold the handle of the hot coffeepot in front of me, taking care not to spill it as I tread on uneven ground. In the other hand, I carry the basket with cups and food behind me so I don't catch it on a plant. Gilbert sneezes from the dust and old pollen that he is knocking off the plants as he charges headlong through the patch. The horses hear the youngster, turn their heads toward the commotion, and snort a greeting.

Thoughts fall in order as I stride toward the wagon. It feels good to walk across the field today. I've been out and about the farmyard, but I haven't been in the fields as I normally am this time of year. Getting back into the open space of the prairie has lifted my spirits. I should have taken this walk sooner.

I delivered Esther last month and have been slow to recover. I've been delayed by my mental health, more so than my physical. After losing two babies, I tend to worry about a new infant's health. I know it is silly because our conditions are so much better than when Josefina and Axel died, yet the depression has lingered. But I know that these feelings can happen to any new mother. Time usually heals the mind as it does the soul. I have five healthy children now, and on this beautiful harvest day, I feel blessed.

I reach for another ear of corn. It was too tempting to be in the field and not snap a few ears. After the men finished their lunch, I placed the coffeepot and basket on the seat of the wagon and joined them as they returned to the rows. I might just as well help pick until the wagon is full. Then we'll ride back to the farmyard with Samuel and Oscar to empty the contents into the corn crib.

I speed up as I get in the rhythm. Twist, snap, throw, bang. Twist, snap, throw, swish. Oops, I overthrew and missed the wagon. Gilbert gleefully runs to retrieve my stray shot. It feels good to be harvesting the dry yellow ears of corn again. They are consistently hefty this year, so we're looking at a good yield.

During our first years, I worked beside Samuel every day to pick our crops. We would shuck corn or cut broom corn from the moment it was dry enough for us to come out to the field in the morning until it was too tough or dark to continue at night.

Our young children came along and played nearby or slept in the wagon. Oscar has spent every fall in the corn fields. He was always upset if he had to start school before the fields were gleaned. Oscar is fourteen this year, so I can no longer force him to go to school. No wonder farming is so important to him. This is all he knows.

As I pick the corn, I compare the cycle of this corn field to my body this year. Last winter the field lay fallow, soaking up the moisture from the snow for the next cycle of planting. Then I was just starting to feel the flutter of life. Spring came, and we prepared the earth and planted the fields with seeds. My clothes grew tight, and my stamina waned as my body changed to adapt to the starting growth of the child.

Summer brought long stretches of sunshine and heat to make the stalks shoot into the air. We cultivated and tended the soil to make healthy plants for harvest. I ate like a horse to sustain the needs of two bodies. I also drank water like an animal that had been in the field all day and sweated like a beast of burden, too.

Now fall is here and I have finished one "harvest," crude as that may sound. I know Esther is blessed with good health, and I'm ready to tackle the rest of the harvest that needs to be done.

After all, this field's crop will feed my own.

1879

Reminiscent Fog

The syrup is starting to thicken, so I continue my watch over the mixture. I stir the sweet-smelling vat of sorghum that is boiling over the open fire pit. We started it hours ago before we began this morning's chores. At first I could occasionally walk by to check it, but now it must be continually stirred so it doesn't burn.

Cane for this batch was harvested yesterday, then pressed to yield the juice. This is the fourth batch I've cooked so far this fall. It takes several gallons of juice to cook down to one gallon of sorghum molasses.

Sugar was expensive in Salina when we arrived here. We looked for honey or grew sorghum for our sweetener. These days we buy sugar, but we still like to make several gallons of sorghum molasses for pancakes.

I add some dried manure to the wood fire to keep it smoldering. The smoke stings my eyes because the weather prevents it from rising. The smell reminds me of our first winter when we burned buffalo chips in the little stove we had in our dugout. It made our home smell like a cow barn. The smoke had a distinct odor and color, but it burned much like coal and lasted much longer than twisted dry grass. We had no choice because no continual wood source was available on the treeless prairie.

From where I stand by the barn, the house barely shows in the gray haze of today's thick fog. Sometimes a clear span shows above or below the blanket of fog, but not today. It's solid from the ground up into the sky. It's past ten o'clock, and the sun hasn't been able to budge it. The fog has layered the earth so thickly that an army could march down the road and I wouldn't see a single soldier.

The distinct wail of a train whistle drifts through the haze. I feel isolated on the farm with the weather closing us in, but hints of the small villages around us still find ways to enter. Tracks for the Kansas Pacific Line have been laid from Salina south through Mentor, Assaria, Bridgeport, Lindsborg, and beyond. It's more than four miles to Assaria, but I can hear the engineer sound his horn.

The Assaria Lutheran Church was the first seedling of that town when the people who lived on the east side of the Smoky Hill River divided with our congregation four years ago. Now Assaria has a train depot, post office, and stores. Bridgeport, three miles farther south, is mostly made up of English settlers. It is a booming town with stores, two hotels, a roller mill on the Smoky Hill River, and a cheese factory. Lindsborg depends on the trade of the area, and the addition of the railroad through it will help it grow.

I don't know if we'll ever get a train line near here. There are two Swedish settlements, Falun and Smolan, west and north of us, but so far they have limited trading possibilities.

The town we trade in depends on our needs. Salina, twelve miles away, has everything we need, but Lindsborg, the other direction and closer by four miles, is becoming a close second. Groceries and mercantile items are obtained at the local villages. I trade eggs and butter for many of our staples.

I look to the south, but still see nothing. The twelve-foot-tall field of broom corn has disappeared beyond the edge of the barn.

We had planned to start cutting broom corn today, but it's too wet. We'll have to wait to see what the weather does. In a minute the sun could break through the clouds and heat up the day, or the clouds could begin a drizzle that could last into tomorrow. Even if the sun comes out, we need lower humidity or the cutting will be tough.

Broom corn is a popular cash crop in our community. Illinois farmers were growing it when we lived there a year, so we were familiar with the crop. Because so many people in this area came from that state, broom corn was one of the first crops planted here. It grows like regular corn, but it doesn't have a corn cob. The seed is in the top tassel. When the stalks dry down in the fall, they are cut and bundled in the field, then hauled to a stripping shed where the seed is scraped from the tops. The bundled tops are shipped to factories in Lindsborg and McPherson, where they are made into brooms.

As I stir the vat, I think about the tasks we must get done before winter hits the plains. Making sorghum molasses is just one of them. Besides harvesting the field crops, the butchering needs to be done.

Fall harvest is different than summer's gathering. Both can be frenzied, but the weather is more likely to hamper the corn and sorghum harvest. The fall offers only a limited time to harvest what has been planted and tended during the summer. A freeze too early in the fall can ruin a crop overnight. Continual wet weather delays cutting the crop and hauling it out of the fields. It also reduces the yield because of spoilage. The seed can sprout in the heads and mold.

Field crops and how they are harvested have changed over the past decade. When we first arrived here, everyone planted sod corn, spring wheat, and potatoes. Our first corn crop was planted by chopping a hole in the sod with the ax and dropping in some seed. When the dry ears were harvested in the fall, we rubbed the hard kernels off the cob with our bare hands, and stored them in burlap sacks hung from the ceiling in our crowded dugout. The corn kernels were ground into meal for cooking, and we burned the empty cobs in the dugout stove.

We didn't plant any spring wheat our first year because we arrived here too late in the season. That crop must be planted in March to be harvested in late summer. A small acreage was planted the next year for chicken feed and our baking needs. We took several bushels to Bridgeport to be ground into flour and meal. Most farmers decided after a few seasons that this type of wheat didn't do well in Kansas. It was susceptible to late spring frosts, which never failed to strike.

A few years after we homesteaded, Russians, who also immigrated to Kansas, introduced a hard winter wheat variety. It is planted in the fall and overwinters to be harvested in the summer. Now instead of harvesting wheat in the fall, we are planting it instead.

Prairie hay was the first forage cut for winter feed when we acquired animals. Large hand-held scythes were used to cut the fields. Now we have a horse-drawn chain mower to cut the tall grass and a hay rake to lay it into windrows. It is hauled in by wagon and stacked in piles by the cattle pens to be used during the winter.

Another forage we grow now for the animals is alfalfa. It can be cut several times during the growing season, depending on the amount of rainfall we get. Weather and timing play a big role in the farmer's luck with his alfalfa. We try to get it cut, dried, and stored in the barn haymow before the rain ruins it. Nothing is worse than seeing fresh-cut alfalfa turned black from rain. It becomes a moldy mess that is not fit to use as feed. And we still have to get the useless feed out of the field so the next cutting can grow.

"Is it done yet?" I jump as Samuel asks the question. He's been working nearby, but I hadn't noticed him stand up and walk toward me and the fire. He had been replacing a wheel on the grain wagon. It had dried out and was starting to squeak. It's better to take it off to soak it in water overnight than to have the rim come off and lose a load of grain somewhere between the field and the barn.

The grain wagon stands in a line with the other farm equipment we have accumulated over the past ten years. We have saved money—or mortgaged a crop—to add equipment, piece by piece, over time. The machinery has made the work easier and made it possible to increase our potential yield and income.

How Samuel longed for the farm machinery we saw on our train trip across America. By now, some of that equipment has become obsolete, and more efficient machinery has taken its place. The Great Plains has been claimed, and equipment is needed to farm it. Manufactories are constantly inventing new machinery to plant and harvest our fields. And Samuel, like a typical farmer, is always eyeing the latest implements when we are in town.

The two-bottom sulky plow has replaced the single walking plow. Much more ground can be covered with three horses pulling and the man riding as compared with the first plow we had that required Samuel to walk behind it and the oxen.

Other equipment has made our work easier. Grain drills plant the corn and wheat seed in several evenly-spaced rows, whereas we used to broadcast by hand or hoe it in. The cultivator works the ground between the rows of growing plants so we don't have to hoe the weeds out of the entire field by hand. The spring tooth harrow rips the ground up after harvest to loosen the soil and work in the stubble. Whoever rides these machines comes in covered with dirt from head to toe, but that is less strenuous than walking behind the equipment all day. And wheat harvest crews now move from farm to farm with their threshing machines instead of the family hand flailing out the seed.

Life is still hard on the farm, but modern machinery has made it much easier and given us the chance to be profitable. It also makes Samuel hungry for more land. He went to Salina last February and completed the claim on this place. Now he is eyeing the land across the road to the north of us.

This batch of molasses is done. I dip a ladle into the nearly empty vat to spoon the thick brown syrup into a tin pail. I set it on an overturned washtub to cool. Steam rises from the container and mixes with the air's thickness. I'll carry it to the food cellar once it cools.

We decide to keep the fire burning and make another batch today. More stalks are pressed, and the yellow-green juice fills the vat again. The hogs grunt with pleasure when Oscar drops the crushed cane into their pen. They had better enjoy their meals while they can, because they will become ham and bacon next month.

After the weather turns cold, we butcher animals for our winter meat supply. We work with neighbors on this big job, taking turns helping with the butchering at each other's farm. Pigs are cut into hams to be smoke-cured, side meat is ground and stuffed in intestinal casings for later use, and the fresh bacon is enjoyed for the first meals after the butchering. Every part—from the blood and organs to the feet—is used in some way for food.

Some people also butcher a steer. This is more work for everyone, so we'll split a half or quarter with neighbors to provide us all some beef. It's a larger animal to hoist, skin, and clean. The meat is usually cooked and canned to be preserved. It isn't smoked like pork. I like to have some because it is nice to have a variety of meat for the winter.

We don't keep sheep for mutton or wool. People here have problems with loss from coyotes and disease. We raised sheep in Sweden for their fleece. It was carded and spun for knitting and material. Now it is cheaper to buy the yarn and fabric instead of raising the animals to supply the raw materials.

During the summer, after our fall meat supply has dwindled, chicken is our main meat source. A young chicken can be scratching in the yard one hour and frying in the skillet the next. Old hens are stewed in soup pots at the end of summer. Along with chickens, goose and turkey eggs are also hatched in the spring. The bigger birds feed more people at a meal when we have company.

By November we are ready for a change in meals and look forward to pork again.

Breathing the sweet smell of sorghum molasses has me thinking of food this morning. Our diet has drastically changed in the past ten years. Meals were simple at first. I cooked what we could find or grow. Many dinners were eaten without bread or coffee. We grew potatoes in our first garden and had them boiled or fried at almost every meal. I didn't have ingredients for cakes or pies, and we longed for something sweet.

I was so hungry for meat our first year. We didn't own any farm animals yet. It was said that a person could have meat if they had a gun and a match. The trouble was, we didn't want to waste a bullet trying to shoot game, and many days it was too windy to light a fire. It was also a waste to shoot large animals during the summer because the meat spoiled so quickly. If a deer or buffalo was shot, only the hind quarters were used and the rest left for the scavengers.

Our main supply of meat was the small animals we could trap on the prairie. I cooked what we caught, whether it be a raccoon or a rabbit. Sometimes I'd get sick of the smell of the cooking game, but I had to feed the family something.

There was a thick population of prairie chickens so we caught one occasionally. It took patience because the shy birds scattered and hid at the least noise. Three nests were secluded in the grass that we watched during the spring. Every few days I took some eggs but always left one so the hen would come back and keep laying. The eggs had a wild taste to them, but they sufficed until we had our own chickens.

I looked for edible plants in the prairie. Tucked among the grasses were wild plants, some that we couldn't identify at first. Maybe they were nutritious greens I could cook up for the family, or maybe a single leaf would poison a child. We had no doctor in our area at that time to help us in such a case, so I used only the plants that I positively knew were safe.

The harvest from my first garden was dried or stored raw. Nothing was canned because we didn't have any crocks or jars, or any space to put them. Dried beans, like the corn, were hung in sacks from the ceiling. Onion tops were left on the bulbs, braided together, and hung within handy reach. Root crops—turnips, carrots, and potatoes—were stored by the dugout in a grass-lined pit dug below the frost line. We dug up what we needed from time to time.

After we built the house, the dugout became our food cellar. Samuel built shelves along the north and south walls to hold jars and a row of bins on the floor beneath them to store the root crops.

The stock has grown larger each year as we have added more vegetables, meat, and now fruit from our orchard. I marvel at the end of each harvest season at how full the shelves are and how bare they will be by the next June.

This season we had several bushels of apples to store in the cellar. The unblemished fruit was wrapped and stored to be eaten fresh during the winter. The majority of the crop was cooked into applesauce, sliced and dried for pies, or pressed into cider. Peaches and cherries were preserved by midsummer. Currants and wild grapes were made into jelly.

Twelve-gallon crocks and large barrels line the east wall. One crock holds pickles in brine, another is filled with homemade apple vinegar fermenting. The other containers are empty and clean, waiting for the butchered meat. Pork sausage, both in patties and casings, will be packed between layers of fat. Other cuts of meat will be placed in barrels and covered with a cooked liquid mixture of salt, brown sugar, and spices. Hams will be hung from the ceiling after they have been cured in the smoke house.

I pick up the pail and walk across the yard to the dugout. As I open the door, a mouse scurries past me. I'll have to let the cat spend some time in here again. We still have problems with creatures claiming the dugout for their own home. It is not unusual to find a potato that has been gnawed by a mouse. More than once I have been surprised by a snake wrapped around a cool crock, or lying on a shelf between a row of jars. We see fewer snakes than we did a decade ago, but they are still around.

The fog still surrounds the farm when I walk out of the dugout. I get a fleeting feeling of the past when I can't see the barn. We were alone on the prairie in the fall of '69, and I was preserving everything I could find for our winter food supply. Our farm has greatly improved since then, but the situation is the same. My life's purpose—taking care of my family—is still tied with growing and preserving food from this land.

Winter

1880

Building Snowflakes

First one, then two. The snowflakes slowly increase in number. We have no wind this morning, so the flakes gently float down to stick to the earth. The dormant trees and shrubs are cold enough that the snow is stacking up on the twigs instead of melting.

Winter is starting late this year. We have had cold spells but no cumulative amount of moisture to go with it. It looks like this soft snow falling today will be the first to completely cover the ground this season.

I lift Esther up in my arms and point at the snowflakes drifting past the dining room window. Last year she was not old enough to understand snow, but this year she is. She looks outside the window, then back at my face. Esther knows the words 'barn,' 'cow,' and such, but doesn't understand 'snowflake.' Her little face looks puzzled as her mind tries to remember an animal that might be called by that name.

Four-year-old Teddy slides up next to us to peer over the windowsill. What is Momma pointing out to his little sister?

"It's snowing, Estie! They're angel flakes!"

He has only seen a few seasons of the winter white, but he remembers what it is. In a flash, his little hands have opened the door, and he's outside twirling around in the flakes. We peer out the open door at his antics, and Esther laughs at her silly brother.

The best way to learn is to show, so we waltz out into the downfall, too. I hold her hand out to catch a flake. She flinches as it hits, but then realizes there is no weight, just a touch of cold before it is gone. Esther lifts her face to the sky. I imagine she is thinking, "What is this stuff that is falling in me?"

Teddy pipes up,"The angels in heaven sprinkle snow on the earth to brighten the brown earth after harvest. It makes things grow next spring."

I had forgotten this story we had told Teddy to explain why snow falls from the sky. He was so full of questions last year that we started making up stories to keep him entertained. Goodness, how will he explain a blizzard to his sister? I can't remember our answer to that question.

By now a few flakes are sticking to my hair. Esther reaches to touch them before they disappear. Instinctively she sticks her fingers in her mouth after feeling the moisture. I stick out my tongue to catch a flake, and she mimics me. She is amused at her new discovery and squeals with delight.

Our last twirl left me facing the house. It dawns on me that I'm finally seeing the old house illustration I had hanging in the dugout. We finally finished the house this fall, and I'm still not used to seeing the new front porch painted.

It has been two years since we started adding on to the house. The two-story addition on the north more than doubles the size of the original frame house.

It seemed as if we were forever in a state of construction and disarray. At times we would spend every spare minute on it, until pressing farm work took precedence, then it would be left untouched for weeks at a time. Help was arranged for jobs that took more than Samuel's and Oscar's strength.

Preparing the basement under the new addition took a month. The food in the dugout was moved into the house and attic, then the sod roof was removed and the walls reinforced. Another room for the basement was dug west of the dugout for a larger space.

When we dug our first home with the hand shovel, it took days of hard-sweating labor. Now the earth was easily moved by the horse-pulled dirt scraper. Two entries were made to get into the basement. The one on the east side of the new addition can be accessed from the outside. That way we can haul garden produce directly downstairs without having to go through the house. The other stairway leads downstairs right off the kitchen from the enclosed porch we added along the east side of the old addition. The house well is also under this porch roof so we can get water in any kind of weather.

Cement powder was purchased and mixed with sand and water to form a cement foundation around the top of the stone basement walls. This ledge was much easier than the uneven rock to build the house frame on.

With delays for harvest and rain, it was the end of October before the first floor was laid.

On the main floor we added a parlor, a kitchen, and a living room. The old north room of the house is now used as the dining room. We added two doors so we can go into either the kitchen or the living room.

Samuel and I still use the old bedroom on the south. The cradle was filled again in October with our latest child, Almeda.

Upstairs we added one large bedroom on the west and two smaller bedrooms on the east. Oscar is in one bed with Gilbert and Teddy sharing the second in the large bedroom. Emily and Esther are in the southeast room. The smallest bedroom is used for the occasional hired man or visitor.

From the upstairs hallway we can still get into the attic in the old section of the house. It's a big step down but still usable. We didn't lath and plaster those walls because the room is used for storage only.

Because of the high hip roof, we have large windows on the west and east walls but only floor windows on the other two sides to aid with air circulation.

The porch for the front of the house leads directly into the parlor. It features a flat roof with a railed balcony around it. It's mostly for show, but a person can get out on the roof from the big window located in the center of the upstairs hallway. I insisted on sturdy railings because the children wanted to sleep out on the porch roof during the summer months, and I wouldn't put it past the boys to try it.

Snow is starting to accumulate on our shoulders, so I shoo Teddy back into the warm house. We didn't stop to put on coats, so we mustn't stay out long. He balks at climbing up the porch steps until I promise hot cider for afternoon lunch. I set Esther down in the high chair by the table so I can fix their snack.

Gilbert slams through the door of the house. He started second grade at Sunny Corner this fall. He is the only child from our family attending school this year because Oscar and Emily have both graduated from eighth grade.

"It snowed all the way home, Momma!" he exclaims. He is just as excited about the snow as the other two. Wait until he grows tired of walking home after a few real snows, and he'll complain instead. He peels off his coat and drops it on the floor on top of his books and slate. He slides into a chair as I carry in a tray of hot cups. I remind Gilbert again to take better care of his school things. Even though he is the third child to use the textbooks, there are three more children who will use them in time.

"Where's your dinner bucket?" asks Emily as she brings the plate of sandwiches into the dining room. "Did you leave it at school again?" Gilbert just shrugs and bites into his sandwich. Dinner is long forgotten as he concentrates on his afternoon lunch.

I think my favorite room in the house is the dining room. Seeing my whole family around the long rectangular table eating my meals is satisfying. With the extra leaves, I have stretched out the table to seat twenty when we've had company. And in a few months, Esther will graduate to a chair so Almeda can use the high chair. Then we'll need eight places for every meal. And to think we started out eating on a crate with two barrels as our only chairs.

Samuel stomps the snow off his boots before entering the house. It's time for his afternoon coffee. I'm glad he comes in during the day to see the children. That is one of the best parts of being a farmer. You are always near your family.

He pauses as he sees us gathered around the table and smiles. What is he thinking? Is he seeing the moment of chatter or realizing that our dream of this house and farm for our family has come true?

1882

Blizzard Milk

I have to lift my leg high to match my boot into Samuel's footsteps in the deep snow. He made the trek to the barn some time ago, and now I'm trying to follow his path. The prints are filling in and becoming hard to find. Oh dear, they disappear in a snow drift that runs horizontal in front of me. My chest tightens with concern. I didn't realize that it was this bad out here. From the frosted window of the house I could see the outline of the barn, but my perspective has changed now that I am in the middle of the storm. Should I go through this drift or go around it? Leaning over to feel it with my gloved hand, I realize it could be waist deep on me. Was this drift here when Samuel came through? Which way did he go if he went around it?

I struggle to keep my balance against the force of the wind. The wind whips my long skirt between my legs, causing me to trip. My half-closed eyes are the only things showing from the scarf wrapped around my head and face. I have on several layers of clothing to protect me, but the sub-zero cold still bites me to the bone. I feel the moisture from my breath freezing in the weave of the cloth that covers my nose and mouth.

So far I haven't found any trace of Esther's shoe size in the snow, but she is so small the tracks would have disappeared by now. Maybe she jumped in Samuel's tracks to the barn as I am doing. Why in the world did she go out in this storm? Samuel said we were all to stay in the house because the storm was so bad. Just he and Oscar went out to do the necessary chores a while ago.

It is hard to tell the late afternoon sky from the ground. It is all a white blur against my stinging eyes. The snow is coming horizontally at such a force that I'm having trouble seeing. The barn vanishes from my sight. It's not far between the house and barn, but I can't see either at this moment. The land slopes down from the house, but I can't feel the drop because of the packed snow. If I go around the drift, I'm afraid I'll wander off course and miss the building altogether. Should I turn around and retrace my steps? I'm guessing I'm halfway between the two buildings. The wind needs to die down long enough so I can see something and get my bearings.

Where is my daughter?! She could have fallen down and been covered over by snow by now or still be wandering around in the blizzard. Is she in one of the outbuildings? How long has Esther been out here? When did she sneak out of the house?

I keep trying to remember. When did I heard the door open and close the second time? The first time it opened, Oscar came in to set the milk pails inside the door. I heard him talking to Esther, then the door shut. I'm sure he went back out to finish chores. When I checked, Emily had picked up the buckets and carried them into the kitchen. Gilbert and Teddy were sitting at the dining room table working on their homework. Esther wasn't there, but I figured she was playing with Almeda in the living room.

A short time later I heard the door again, and I thought Oscar had finished his outside duties and was back inside. Only later when I heard Almeda fussing did I realize she was alone and Esther wasn't in the house. My only clue to her whereabouts was one of her mittens lying by the back door.

Why haven't Samuel and Oscar come back from the barn yet? It shouldn't have taken so long to finish chores. Why can't I see the light from the barn lantern? It usually glows bright at night from the east window of the building. Maybe we missed each other in the poor conditions, and they are back in the house wondering where I am. Is Esther with them?

Should I turn around and head back to the house?

This blizzard reminds me of the weather we had a decade ago. It lasted from early winter until March of '72. All winter we fought sleet, sheets of ice, and snow drifts from eight to fifteen feet tall. It was an exhausting struggle to keep the livestock fed and watered. I thought the spring thaw would never come. Of course when it did, we had knee-deep mud in the animal pens. We lost several calves that winter due to the poor weather. The conditions were too harsh for them.

We had one blizzard in '70 that was deadly. That was before we built the house and barn. It was cold in the dugout, but we were insulated from the elements. The bad part of that winter was having to go out to check our only cow. She was tied up in an open lean-to made of hay piled up to form a north wall and roof. She was a brown cow, but you couldn't tell that from the deep blanket of ice and snow that layered her back. We had to dig her out before she suffocated from the packed snow. We tried moving her into the dugout with us but didn't have any luck. She was so cold and fatigued she wouldn't budge. We should have tried harder, because the below-zero blizzard froze the poor animal where she lay. We spent the rest of that winter without milk.

Maybe the men are in the corral trying to move the livestock in through the back door of the barn. They couldn't fit them all in, but at least the young stock could be sheltered. It seems that if Esther had found them, Oscar would carry her back to the house instead of waiting until they were done. She took her coat and hat, but they aren't warm enough to be much protection in this blizzard. And I know one little hand is unprotected without its glove.

This snow started early this morning. I had to brush a thick layer off the wooden seat in the outhouse before using it. The wind was blowing flakes into every crack visible in the little building, and it had accumulated an inch deep inside.

The animals were slow to stir this morning when we went out to do chores. Instinct told them to huddle against the storm to keep warm. I intended to do the same once every creature had been taken care of.

I checked the chicken house on the way to the barn. The birds ruffled their feathers and shivered as the cold blast hit them when I opened the door. The hens hadn't flown down from their roosts to eat or nest yet today. The rooster sat among the hens. I didn't hear a crow out of him this morning. After I closed the door, I peeked around the corner of the building to make sure the side door was latched. It was too cold to let the chickens out in their pen today.

It was difficult getting into the barn this morning. We all did different tasks before heading to the barn, so each of us had to struggle with the door. Samuel heard me trying to get in and finally came to my rescue. The force of the wind was holding it shut because the door rolls to the north.

Our dog, Johan, laid curled up by the door. His nose was buried in his tail that curved around his body. He would have been warmer away from the door, but he had to see what was going on. It was only open a crack, but it was just enough that he could look out over the yard. He raised his head when he heard Oscar approaching the barn and thumped his tail when the boy came in the door and patted his head, but his nose went right back into his fur as soon as Oscar passed him.

Tied in their stalls, the draft horses turned their heads to eye Oscar and the bucket of oats he dipped out of the grain bin. Their breath formed a cloud around their heads. One lifted his tail and dropped fresh manure on the floor. Heat and smell rose from the pile until it cooled. It is so cold in the barn today that it froze within the hour.

I lifted the milking stool off its hook on the wall, sat down on it next to first cow, put the freezing cold metal pail between my knees, and started coaxing milk from the cow's teats. I leaned against the animal's side for warmth. I couldn't believe how cold it was today, even inside the protection of the barn. At least the warm stream of milk warmed up the bucket for me. Even though there is less milk production during winter, it took longer than usual to milk this morning because of my cold hands. The frothing milk was as white as the snow outside today. It looks so different now than in the summer time when the fresh greens the cows eat turn the milk a creamy yellow.

The cats stayed in the protection of the barn's hay pile during this morning's commotion. After I milked the first cow, I poured some of the warm liquid into their pan for their breakfast. They rushed to lap it up, then crawled back into the cozy holes. I noticed that by the time I had moved to the third cow the little bit of milk left in the bottom of the pan had turned to ice.

Chores done, Samuel slid the barn door open just enough so we could carry the milk buckets out sideways through the opening. The wind caught the door and threatened to blow it off its track again. This time out Samuel latched the door shut against the storm. The dog whined in protest, but we must protect the livestock from the storm.

Snow twirled around me going back to the house. Samuel and Oscar followed me, each carrying a bucket of milk.

It felt so good in be back in the warmth of the house. After we shook the snow from our outer garments and hung them up to drip and dry, we sat down to a hot breakfast. My hands, cupping the coffee mug, smarted as the blood seeped back into my numb fingers, but the hot liquid thawed me from the inside out.

All signs indicated today's weather was going to turn dangerous for both man and beast. Samuel decided that the children should stay home from school and made the point of saying all of us should remain in the house until it was time to do chores again this afternoon.

The lid to one of the school dinner pails is stuck in the drift in front of me. What is it doing out here? Did Esther have it with her? Why?

I hear the dog barking. Suddenly the barn looms in front of me, and I lunge for the door. It won't budge. It must be locked from the inside this time. Pounding with my clinched fists, my thumping is answered by Oscar opening the door wide enough to let me in.

"Is Esther with you? She left the house a while ago, and I can't find her!"

"She was in the house when I took in the milk," he answers.

"Did she say anything? We need to find out where she is!" My voice rises in impatience and fright as my oldest son shakes his head.

"She just asked if I had fed the cats, and I said no, put the buckets down, and came back to the barn."

That's it! The dinner pail lid! Esther probably filled it with milk from the fresh bucket and went out to feed her silly cats! But she didn't make it to the barn. Where is she? It's too cold out here for her to survive alone.

Johan sticks his head out between the door and my skirts and barks into the blinding whiteness. Does he know where Esther is?

"Where's Esther, Johan? Find Esther!" I don't know if the dog can understand me, but he knows I'm upset about something.

He sniffs the lid still in my hand, then bounds past me into the snow. Is he looking for a pail of fresh milk for his own drink, or does he know of its connection with Esther? I chase after the dog, quickly losing sight of him but continuing to follow his fresh tracks and his occasional noise. He leads me toward the chicken house. Feeling around to the east of the little building I find that the door latch is still in place. Johan sniffs around the corner into the open pen gate on the south side.

There! On the side of the building is a dribble of cream, frozen where it was sloshed against the siding. Esther must have been here recently.

Chickens squawk with the intrusion of the barking dog. How did he get inside the chicken house? Struggling through the drift that has wrapped around the building, I see only his body sticking out of the two-foot-high door that the chickens use to enter the pen.

Going back to the east door, I open it wide enough to peek in. In the corner, covered with snow, hay, and feathers, sits Esther, shivering, still clutching the container holding her kitties' supper!

1883

Riding Ice

From the parlor window, I see Hedda pull her team up to the house. As soon as she stops the horses, her three children pile out of the sleigh and join their cousins playing in the front yard. Snowballs have flown by the parlor window for the past hour as Mathilda's and my children entertain themselves. The two sides renew their battles from the protection of their snow forts with new recruits. Now there are nine youngsters playing in the snow, the boys outnumbering the girls five to four.

Oscar and Emily step out the door now that Carl, Hedda's stepson, is here. The three older children have plans of their own today, and they set off in our sleigh to a sledding party on the buttes.

Dinner dishes are done, and we women are ready to leave. Mathilda and I gather our cloaks and head out the door ourselves, giving instructions to Samuel and Lars that will largely be ignored. They will sit and visit all afternoon and not pay a bit of attention to their children playing outdoors. There are two three-year-olds out there who should come in for a nap soon, but I know that might be impossible with so many playmates today.

Mathilda and her family are visiting us this weekend for an early Christmas reunion. They want to be at their own church for their Sunday school program and early Christmas morning service, so they decided to come now. They traveled by train from Enterprise to Assaria, and Samuel picked them up at the depot yesterday evening. Hedda and her family arrived at our house shortly afterward so we could eat supper together and start visiting.

Today is my thirty-ninth birthday so my two sisters put their heads together last night and decided we should do something special, just we three sisters, without the whole lot of children tagging along. Mathilda voted to go shopping in Lindsborg, and Hedda offered to drive their sleigh. I protested that, being eight months pregnant, I didn't care to be seen in public, but my arguments fell on deaf ears.

Our main purpose of this trip is to buy some "American" gifts for our family in Sweden. Mathilda and Julia plan to sail back for a visit in the coming year, and we'll send these gifts along with them. Now is a good time to buy because the stores have nice selections for the holidays. And I think we all have Christmas shopping we still need to do, too.

I must write to our parents about this weekend when it is over. They enjoy hearing the antics of their grandchildren and would be pleased to know that all their American family was together to celebrate the holidays. Maybe we should buy a nice Christmas card for them today. Everyone, including the children, could sign it while we are all in one place. Both Samuel's parents and his step-mother are gone, so my father and mother are the only grandparents left for my children to communicate with.

We've kept in touch with my parents through letters. Even though Father's handwriting is deteriorating, he keeps scribbling back to us, exclaiming joyfully at the simple stories we write about our family and farm. It's hard to see the change in his letters and imagine our parents aging, but it has been fifteen years since we left Sweden.

What would Father think of his 'Lotta, Hedda, and 'Tilda, driving to town in such a handsome sleigh as this? Oh, he would be so proud to see us all decked out in our fine coats and fancy winter hats, riding in style behind this matching team of horses.

It is a beautiful winter day. The sun shines overhead as we turn out of the lane. Snow is melting off the roof and adding icicles to the trim on the house. Yesterday's new layer lies level with the ground, covering the landscape with an incredible brilliance.

The sleigh runners barely cut through the new snow, and we slide along at a smooth pace. The horses are frisky from the cold and strain to go faster than a gait as we travel the eight miles to Lindsborg.

Snow covers the fields that lie sleeping until spring. Farms dot the white landscape at regular intervals. Some are near the road, and others can be seen at a distance. The trail follows a rock fence along the front of some acreages, just as the roads did in the old country. We Swedes had hoped to never see another stone again, but unfortunately there are parts of this valley land that are rocky.

The party that our young people joined is in full swing on top of the hill to the southwest of us. It is a popular place for sledding. It's a long walk up, but a person can slide almost a half mile down once they start. A toboggan holding five people just careened off track, spilling its passengers along the way. The large sled continues down the hill empty. A bonfire at the base of the slope warms the group before they ascend the hill again. We can hear the laughter of the group above the noise of our jingling harness.

We had many hills to slide down when we were children. Our sleds were crude, but we had just as much fun. And lakes to skate on. Some people skate on the river here, but it just isn't the same. Some pastimes are the same for young people wherever they live, and others are different for the same reason.

Our lives turned out so differently than what we had planned when we were young. None of us thought we would stray far from home, much less to another continent.

Hedda traveled with my family from Sweden to Kansas, then married a local man. But Mathilda worked in Chicago before coming to Kansas. She also hired out in Topeka, Salina, and Abilene before her marriage to Lars Jaderborg.

Her wedding was an unusual one. Lars, who farms northeast of Enterprise, came to Kansas in '58 after three years in Illinois. He worked as a blacksmith in the area until the Civil War. Lars traveled around with the Second Kansas Calvary, then came back to his original claim when the war ended.

Bachelors often hire women to come out to their farms to do the washing and cook up a supply of meals. Mathilda occasionally went to Lars' homestead to work for him. One day while she was at the washtub scrubbing his clothes, he came up to her and said the preacher had arrived. Would she marry him today? If not, he had another girl in mind. Lars is twenty-one years older than Mathilda, but she decided he was as good a man as any, so she took off her apron and married him on the spot. Lars has done well for his family. They lived in the log cabin for two years, then built a nine-room stone house.

Mathilda had twin girls in '75, but only Julia survived. Son Thure was born two years later. Another daughter, Ida, born in '81, died in November last year.

The children in our three families, except for my Oscar and Emily, are all similar in age. Hedda's Axel is nine now; she also has a daughter named Esther who is seven, and her youngest, John, is three. Her last child, Augusta, died last June on the day she was born. The two Esthers and Julia are becoming the best of friends and mirror the three of us sisters when we were growing up.

"What would Father like best, the blue scarf or the red one?" Hedda asks as she holds up the two items. We decide on red, Hedda pays for the purchase, and we move on to the next store.

We wander through the stores downtown, enjoying the freedom of the afternoon away from our families. In one store, a child says "Momma," and all three of us automatically turn around. We laugh, acknowledging we are still mothers at heart, as well as sisters out on a shopping spree.

For our mother we purchase several yards of fine white material, embroidery floss in a variety of colors, two packages of fine needles, and a metal embroidery hoop. She likes to do handwork and will enjoy having materials to make some new table runners or pillow cases.

Books and sheets of music are on Oscar and Emily's wish list, so I find their gifts at the book store. I pick out toys for

Gilbert's and Teddy's presents at the novelty shop. I have already made doll clothes for Esther and Almeda, but I buy each of them a length of new hair ribbon to wear at the Christmas church program.

Samuel can be hard to buy for, but Oscar told me of a hand tool that his father had been wanting, so another purchase is made at the hardware store.

Our last stop is the grocery store. The scents of oranges, cinnamon bark, and peppermint oil meet us at the door. Displays crowd the room. Fresh fruit, a bin of whole nuts, cans of oysters, cones of sugar—it is stocked to the ceiling with treats for the holiday. All the American and Swedish favorites are available.

What a contrast today's Christmas shopping—and selection—has been compared to our first years here. An orange would have been a child's only gift—if we had walked to Salina to buy it and had the money to do so. Now we buy a gift for everyone in our family, bake special treats and deliver holiday baskets to neighbors, and celebrate the whole season long with parties and church festivities. We are no longer isolated in a prairie dugout celebrating the birth of Jesus. Now we do it together with family and friends.

The sun is sinking behind the buttes as we start home. The clouds topping the hills are dark gray but a bright yellow halo shines above them. The white smooth snow on the road has turned to gray-blue ice from the day's traffic. The sledding party has been abandoned because most of the young people had to go home to do the evening chores.

The lights shining from my home are warm and inviting as we turn into our lane. It has been a fun afternoon, but my feet are swollen, and I am tired. I am ready to be home, back on the farm with my family.

1884

Frozen Memories

Another son! Hedda lays the newborn on my chest, and I stare at the little pink body. He's quiet but seems to be perfect in form. I touch his little cheek with a finger and marvel at his delicate skin. Another fair-skinned farmer. Before long he'll look like the rest of my boys after spending days out in the field—red cheeked, with a white forehead.

Emily drapes a blanket over her new brother to protect him from the cold draft. Because of the labor, I hadn't noticed that the early January morning had cooled the room.

I'm exhausted from the night's labor and close my eyes for a minute. But I feel one weight, then another, crawling onto the other side of the bed. I'm guessing my two little girls have sneaked into the room and climbed in to examine the baby. I open my eyes to be greeted by my husband and six children surrounding me. Samuel leans over to kiss my sweaty forehead, then picks up his new son, Joseph Nathanial, to pass around the family.

Teddy, elbow against the table, wearily holds his head up in his hand. He has been stirring his porridge this morning rather than eating it. He looks as if he doesn't feel well. I cup my hand around his forehead. It's hot. I hope he's not coming down with a cold. The children just started back to school yesterday after their Christmas break. I hate for him to miss classes, but I think he needs to go back to bed rather than out into the winter air.

Teddy doesn't protest at the suggestion. He slides out of his chair and drags his feet toward the stairs. Gilbert, full of energy this morning, bundles up in his coat, hat, and scarf, and gets ready to charge out the door. I hand him his dinner pail and remind him to bring Teddy's schoolwork home this afternoon. My two young boys are usually a matching pair, but there is a marked difference today.

I sit on the edge of the bed listening to Teddy's breathing. I just put a mustard plaster on his chest, trying to loosen the congestion and ease the coughs that rattle his body. I hope he does not get worse overnight. Gilbert crawls in bed beside his brother and promptly nestles down in the quilts. Hopefully both will have a good night's sleep.

I tiptoe into the girls' room to check on them. Esther and Almeda each have a doll wrapped in their arms. They have been playing with their "babies" this week, imitating me and their new baby brother. I feel a pang of guilt because I haven't had as much time to spend with them recently. I lean over the sleeping children to kiss them good night. Almeda's forehead seems warm, and I check it again. I hope she isn't coming down with a cold, too.

As Almeda struggles for another breath of air, I hold my own, hoping that this won't be her last. The doctor couldn't help, so it is up to God to decide the fate of my child. I wipe her feverish face with a cold cloth, peering into her dull eyes, trying to see any improvement. I can't break down now. I have to be here for her. I had to abandon Teddy's lifeless body last night, and I fervently pray that Almeda doesn't succumb to diphtheria also.

Samuel's tear-stained face leans over the bed. He touches his daughter's chest to feel if it is still rising, then he wraps his arms around me and pulls me off the bed. "The pastor is here to baptize the baby. It needs to be done now in case Joseph . . . ." Samuel can't finish the sentence. All babies must be baptized to be able to enter heaven. It is usually done at the church unless there is reason to believe the infant won't survive. If the pastor isn't available, a midwife might perform the baptism at birth to save the child's soul. And with a deadly disease in the house, Joseph must be given the rites without delay.

Teddy passed away in my arms on the eighteenth of January and Almeda on the nineteenth. Normally someone would have gone to town right away to buy a casket—but with a second child lingering close to death, there was a strong possibility we needed two. That happened Saturday night, so we had to wait until Monday to go to town.

For the interim, Samuel took down the parlor door and rested it across chairs in the room. Bedding and pillows were piled on top, then we laid the little bodies in their Sunday best on the door.

We covered their faces and hands with cloths dipped in saltpeter to keep their skin from discoloring. We didn't light the parlor stove. It was best to keep the bodies cold.

Early this morning Oscar drove the wagon to town, his father sitting like stone next to him. It was afternoon before they returned.

Samuel spared no expense for the burial of his children. In the back of the wagon were two pine boxes. Inside each was a hand-crafted coffin of dark walnut wood, with a window in the lid. I couldn't help but compare the differences in the burials of our four children. The first two children we lost were buried in cruder boxes than the shipping crates that held these beautiful caskets.

Samuel also stopped at a clothing store and bought white burial outfits for each one. I was so surprised. I hadn't thought of this or mentioned it to him. Did his conscience bother him about the pitiful way we laid Josephina and Axel to rest? Whether a family is rich or poor, it doesn't matter—death can still knock on the door.

We changed the clothes on the stiff bodies and laid them in their coffins. Almeda fit perfectly, Teddy's coffin could have been a size larger. Gilbert polished their shoes. Emily tied a white ribbon in Almeda's hair. In each set of hands we tucked a sprig of white silk flowers. I wish we would have had fresh ones, but that's the best we could do in January.

So now I'm spending every minute I can, sitting between the caskets of my children. I shut my eyes and trace their hair and face with my hands to memorize their features. Tomorrow they will be laid to rest, and I'll never see their faces again. I want to be able to close my eyes and remember them again.

The ribbons of the death badges whip in the wind outside the parlor door. One is always placed on the front door to show that the family is in mourning: black ribbons for an adult, black and white for an adolescent, and white for a child. We have two white crepe badges on our door.

I try to hold back the tears as I watch Esther talking to Almeda. She has her sister's favorite doll in her hand, and she is holding it so Almeda can see it. The contrast is too much to bear. A lively little five-year-old, bundled up in winter clothing to ward off the chill in the parlor, chatting away to her three-year-old sister, who is lying in a coffin, dressed in summer white.

Theodore, died January 18, 1884   *Almeda, died January 19, 1884*

This is going to be so hard on Esther and Gilbert. Almeda and Teddy were close to their own ages, so they each had someone to play with. Oscar and Emily are so much older that they seem more like parents to the younger children. Now Esther's choice of playmates is a brother five years older than she is, or an infant brother almost six years younger.

In less than two weeks' time, I gave birth to one child and lost two. And why Teddy and Almeda? And how were the others spared? I shudder when I realize we could have been burying more than two tomorrow.

The day is bleak and cold. The photographer motions us into position. He suggested that a family portrait be taken in front of the house while he is here. The man asks about the baby, but I tell him that Joseph was left inside rather than risk his health in the cold air.

Our dark mourning clothes contrast with the skiff of white snow that fell on the prairie last night. We stand braced against the cold and the day's misery. Esther stands first on one foot, then

Johnson family in front of their house

the other. I take hold of her hand to keep her still long enough to have our picture taken.

The photo will show how well this Swedish immigrant family has done on this land, but every time I look at it, I will think of the four children who never had the chance to grow up on this farm.

While Samuel was in Salina, he commissioned a photographer to come out to the farm before the burial. This was our last chance to have a memento taken of Teddy and Almeda. I still regret we couldn't do that for Josefina and Axel. After fourteen years, their faces have blurred in my mind, so I know we have to do this to remember Teddy and Almeda.

After he has taken pictures of the caskets, he sets up a backdrop in the corner of the parlor and takes photos of our other children. It will cost extra, but life has taught us that children may not last as long as the money we are trying to save for them.

Oscar and Emily

A wagon is pulling up to the house. No, two. I glance at the clock. People are starting to arrive for the two o'clock funeral.

The news of our children's deaths was announced in church Sunday. I can imagine the gasps and stricken faces that followed. Just two weeks prior, Samuel had taken the children to church while I was at home with the new baby.

Another group of buggies and wagons turns in. The men will let their families off by the front door, then drive toward the barn to tend to their horses. Hushed noises drift down the hall as the first mourners enter the house.

This is my last minute alone with my children. I kiss each child on the lips and stroke their hands one last time. Then I raise my head and straighten my back to receive the visitors.

Tearful women bravely enter, carrying dishes of food, offering murmurs of condolences, giving hugs of passion. Shy children follow behind, scared but curious to see their playmates lying motionless in the parlor. Solemn men come last, dreading to reveal emotion but needing to show support.

Several of our neighbors have been through this same kind of loss. Sandberg's daughter, Hulda, died last October. Johan and Christina Thelander have lost three toddler sons. We helped them through the pain then, so now they in turn help us.

Voices singing "Children of the Heavenly Father" echo through the house. Our immediate family is seated in the parlor for the funeral, but people are standing in the hall and every other room downstairs for the service. Today we're not alone on the prairie saying good-bye to our dead. This time our community surrounds us.

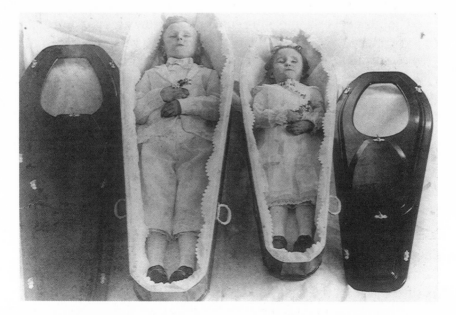

Theodore and Almeda, buried January 22, 1884

After the final verse, the lids are set on the coffins and locked in place. Neighbors carry them out to the waiting wagon. As I walk out the door, I realize I will come back to this house, but two of my children will never step across this threshold again.

The church bell tolls slowly for one child, stops for a long silent minute, then tolls for the other. The bell has rung for every church service and funeral since it was put up three years ago. I heard it from our bedroom the Sunday morning I gave birth to Joseph. The sound rang loud and clear through the crisp January air. At the time I remember thinking, what a joyful way to announce the birth of a new infant. Now the bell is ringing again for two more of my family but for a sadder reason.

This is the first grave used in our family plot at the church cemetery. When we originally bought this plot, I imagined our children standing here burying us first, not the other way around.

The grave diggers had to use pick axes to slice through the frozen ground. They made only one hole to hold both small coffins. Now both rough pine boxes rest in the bottom of the hole, waiting to receive the coffins as they are committed.

Clouds cover the morning sun, but no snow or wind threatens us—just the unforgiving cold that we cannot stop. We form a tight circle around the two coffins sitting next to the hole in the ground. Our family, Hedda's, neighbors. It is as if we are trying to hold the winter cold from chilling the coffins, but it is too late for the bodies encased in wood.

After Pastor Dahlsten's closing prayer, I watch the faces of my children through their glass windows as the pallbearers move on both sides of the hole. Using long harness reins tied together, they gently lower first Almeda's casket, then Teddy's, into the waiting boxes. When they are in place, the reins are pulled out, and the men step back to stand behind the family. The grave digger crawls into the hole, and another man hands him a lid, hammer, and nails. One last glance, then I turn away as the tool is raised to nail the first lid down.

Oscar steps up and removes the lid of the dinner pail he has been holding during the service. It is actually an old syrup can with a handle, but he first carried it to school as his dinner pail twelve years ago, then it was passed down to Teddy when he was ready to start last year. It is full of dents, has held countless sandwiches, and was swung miles by growing arms.

Today it holds the symbol of the land where his siblings were born and where they died. Tipping the can, he pours a little soil into each of our hands. We needed earth to commit the bodies, and Oscar suggested we use soil from our farm. He chipped frozen clods from the burial corner of our land, then warmed and dried them in the kitchen oven so we could have earth to pour into the graves.

Samuel and I pour the farm's earth on the coffins first. Gilbert tosses his soil onto Teddy's box. Esther, reluctant to let go of the soil, finally pours most of her handful on Almeda's. The rest she keeps in her gloved hand, cupped to her chest. Emily outlines the shape of the cross on each box.

Oscar has given the rest of us soil but didn't take any out for himself. There is plenty left over since he brought the pail full. He reaches into his pocket, pulls out his bulging handkerchief, and empties its content in the soil.

Rye—descended from the grain that was first planted in the corner of our farm fifteen years ago. Does Oscar remember us planting that seed and watching it grow? He was only five at the time. Perhaps he remembers burying Josefina and Axel next to the rye plot a year later—or the countless trips I made to visit their graves that fall.

Oscar dips his hand in the bucket to stir the mixture, then pours a generous handful on each box. Apparently for his own peace of mind, he needs to tie the two burial plots and our farm land together.

We leave when the grave diggers have filled the hole halfway. When we get to the buggy I notice Oscar is not with us. I look back to see him still standing alone by the hole, waiting for the men to finish their job.

He has been reserved today, quietly keeping his thoughts to himself. I wonder, being the oldest, does he feel as if he's the keeper of his younger siblings?

Today is January 22, Oscar's twentieth birthday. I hate having to bury Teddy and Almeda on this day, but we can't wait any longer.

Oscar has passed into manhood and will soon be on his own. What will the future hold for him and his family? Will he have to stand near this same site and watch some of his own children be buried, too?

The grave diggers are done. They pick up their equipment and leave. Oscar takes the lid off the pail again and carefully covers the grave mound with the rest of the pail's contents. He stoops to smooth and pat the grain into the mound. With this act, he has planted Teddy and Almeda's last field.

I sigh as I realize I did it again. A week has passed since the funeral, and I'm still setting the table for too many places. I'm doing the same when cooking our meals. Too much porridge, too many potatoes. Being young, they didn't seem to eat much, but it does make a difference.

On the table beside the door sits Teddy's last homework. We've all ignored the pile, not wanting to disturb it. Gilbert brought it home the day Teddy became ill, laid it down in his usual rush to raid the kitchen pantry, and Teddy never recovered to work on his studies.

There are so many reminders around the house of the two children. Their coats hanging by the back door. Teddy's toy iron horse we gave him for Christmas. I can still smell their individual scents on their clothing. They had personalities, identities all their own, that will never be duplicated. And right now, I don't want to disturb their things or their memories.

"Look, Momma! Teddy and Almeda are sending down their angel flakes!" Esther remarks from her stance by the window. I look down at my daughter in amazement. How does she connect the story Teddy told her about snow with the siblings she just lost? "You said they went to heaven, so these flakes must be from them!"

In a second she scoots out the door with me tailing behind in hot pursuit. I'm automatically thinking, "It's freezing outside;

she doesn't have a coat on; I can't let her get sick; I can't lose another child!"

"Hello, Hello? Can you hear me?" Esther stands in the middle of the yard, her face turned to the sky, her arms reaching out to catch the snowflakes falling gently down. "Almeda! Teddy! It's me!"

I stop short, then crumble to the ground in shock. Oh, it hurts, it hurts so badly. I wail uncontrollably at the realization that Teddy and Almeda are gone forever. I will never be able to tuck them into bed again, scold them for not eating the food I prepared for their meal, give them another hug. How can I face the sorrow and guilt? What if it happens again?

A little arm slips around my neck, and a small hand pats my shoulder. I look up to see Esther's fair head covered with a halo of snow.

"Momma, you said Teddy and Almeda are watching over us. Isn't that true?" Her delighted face at seeing the snowflakes has changed as she worries about my reaction.

I wipe my tears, then gather her to me for a tender hug. "Oh, yes, it's true, Esther. Momma wouldn't lie to you."

I turn my tearful face towards my angels' flakes and try not to cry again. I still have five children who need me.

Esther

Spring

1885

Healing Rain

It looks as if it could start raining at any moment. I study the soft clouds that are hanging low in the sky this afternoon. These are the type that gently release their moisture, not the thunderheads that battle each other with noise and flashes. Will we be in luck today, or will the clouds change their minds?

I step off the east porch to empty the basin of wash water on the patch of irises behind the house. The buds are starting to show a deep purple on the tight points. Another few days and I'll have a bed full of delicate lavender blooms. Wild violets crowd around the bases of the iris plants. Their tiny flowers stand above the heart-shaped violet leaves and offer up a sweet fragrance to the air.

Spring has crept up on me. I have been busy with spring cleaning this week and haven't noticed the changes in nature these past few days. I've been in and out of the house, hanging the rugs and curtains on the clothes line, but I haven't stopped long enough to see that the perennials were beginning to flower.

It took longer to give the house a thorough cleaning this spring. I hate to admit it, but I was used to Emily doing half the work. She is on her own this spring, working in Brookville at a hotel. So, that left Esther and me to do the work. I couldn't expect a lot of help from my six-year-old, but she did simple tasks. I'm patient with her because this is how she will learn to take care of her own house someday.

The orchard trees are in full bloom. The light pink apricot trees are always first, followed by the peach. The white blossoms are the cherry trees. The apple blossoms vary in color and timing depending on the variety of tree. Why didn't I see this show of color before? I guess I was looking at smudges on the window panes instead of looking through the glass at the swelling buds.

I wander out to the garden to see if anything has sprouted yet. A gentle rain this afternoon would give it a good start. We soaked the peas before dropping them in their rows so they should be peeking out of the ground soon. The tiny wisps of the first onion seed are showing if I look down the row just right. The cabbage plants were set out a month ago and are already gaining in size. The ground is still fluffy and undisturbed around the rows except where children, pets, or chickens have walked through it.

I continue my walk to check the flowers and shrubs. What about the lilac bushes on the north side of the house? I wonder what stage the flower buds are at. The last time I looked there were just tiny bits of green starting to grow. Now the new leaves cover the branches of the lilacs. The clusters on the end of the stems will expand into fragrant groups of lilac flowers by the first of May.

A bit of faded cloth is snagged among the base branches of one shrub. I retrieve the fragment and recognize the texture as soon as I touch it. It is white crepe, shredded and stained from the weather, a remnant of the death ribbons that hung on our house.

It has been three months since I removed the tattered ribbons from our front door. They hung there for a whole year, through four seasons of weather, before I took down what was left of the decoration. Usually they are removed within a few weeks of the funeral, but it didn't feel right to erase the symbol of our mourning from the house so soon. Every time I left the farm, then came back home, I would see the ribbons on the front porch door and remember the double blow of death that had hit our home.

I finally went out at two o'clock on the afternoon the 22nd of January to remove the ribbons. It was a private act that I wanted to do alone, to say a final good-bye to Teddy and Almeda.

When I took down the ribbons, detailed memories from that week flooded my mind. I relived my childrens' struggle for their last breaths and the silences that followed. Shutting my eyes I could trace their little faces, feel their down-fine hair. And when I opened my eyes, my mind flashed back to the first shovelful of soil being thrown into the hole that held their coffins.

Being their mother, I would have sacrificed my own life to spare theirs, but that wasn't how God planned it. It took time to accept that fact and heal the pain.

I stood on the porch and cried until I had no tears left. The cold prairie wind froze my falling grief and eased my pain. The year had passed for mourning, and I felt as if a huge weight had been lifted from my spirit.

I still look at Teddy's and Almeda's portraits almost daily. It might seem morbid to some people, but to me it is a comfort to see their little faces again. Every month on the days and hours that they died, I have stopped what I was doing and silently thought of them for a moment. Even though they are gone, they will always be my little children, and I won't ever forget them.

I wander past the house and the orchard to the grave site in the northeast corner of our farm. The new grass is green and lush among last year's dead growth that had melted down from the weight of winter. This corner is not mowed so the grass reaches its full potential in the fall.

Wild and domestic flowers will begin their displays on this site before long, and I am curious to see if anything has started yet. No matter what month I come out here during the growing season, there is something blooming for me to enjoy. I tended the graves for years, but the prairie slowly took over the care of the mounds, so I retreated to become a viewer again.

The purple sweet rocket I originally planted reseeds itself each year. They are an early flower, and I see their tall blooming stalks as I walk over to the site.

Irises, matching the variety by the house, mix with the fuzzy mounds of yarrow. One solitary iris flower is open. This patch started blooming before the one by the house this year even though I have been watering the latter occasionally.

The bright pink petals of the wild roses will add another color before long. Then the white yarrow, followed by orange day lilies and several types of cone flowers. Frost asters, goldenrod, and late sunflowers will finish the grave blanket in the fall.

A wild plum thicket stands guard along the north side of our boundary line. Its white blossoms are so thick that it looks as if a person could fall into its cushion of softness. But nature is deceiving. The bushes wrap themselves in a fortress of thorns to protect their fruit, much like a mother protects her children. She may look like a frail individual, but she is tough on the inside.

Droplets bead on the iris petals as the mist turns heavier. Gentle rain falls silently on the grass and drips off the blades to water the soil. I breathe in the scent of fresh rain. I look out to see the steady decent of the shower. I should go back to the house, but at the moment I'm taking pleasure in this spring rain.

This corner is where I finally learned to embrace the beauty of nature. We must enjoy things while we have them, whether it is for an hour or for a lifetime. Nature can destroy with storms or disease, but it always gives life back to the earth with its next season.

There have been four deaths on this piece of prairie. But they were all part of the cycle of life on this land. We were the first to plant on this farm; we won't be the last.

But I hope the end of my cycle is a long time coming, because I'm not done with this prairie yet.

1886

Lifting Breezes

The screaming birds swirl in the air, then drop from the sky to follow Samuel and the team as they plant the field of corn. The pure white birds with the black-tipped wings are looking for grain just seeded and for insects and worms that have been overturned in the process. How and why do sea gulls find their way to the Kansas prairie? How do they know when it is time to plant?

Samuel is at the far end of the field, so I stop to wait for him to make the round back to me. At least he is easy to locate when I come out with his forenoon coffee. I just look to the sky for his location.

I notice that Samuel's shoulders are starting to stoop, although he is still a towering man. There isn't a touch of gray under his straw hat, but his beard is starting to show age. His big hands guide the reins of the horses with simple gestures. He is concentrating on driving in a straight line and doesn't even notice the birds that circle him. Nor do the horses seem to care.

The bird's noisy call is the same as I remember it when we stood on the pier in Göteborg harbor. We were a young, naive couple planning to start over in America. And we did just that. We cultivated hope into this land, and it has multiplied for our children.

The soft breeze flutters my sunbonnet back from my face. The touch of today's wind is gentle and warm. I don't mind the wait because the spring weather is perfect today. I sink down to the earth. I can feel the warmth of the heated field through my skirt.

I pick up a handful of soil and rub it between my fingers and my palm. The moisture is just right for planting. The seed should germinate right away. I lift it to my nose. The smell of warm earth is comforting. I love this prairie we call home.

I hated this land for a while when we first settled here. Life was harder than I imagined it would be. But I couldn't quit just because I was tired or scared. I had a family to care for, and I had no choice but to plant and harvest the land we had chosen for our home. I swallowed complaints, learned patience, and prayed that our hard work would not be defeated by the weather.

My attention returns to the gulls again. The clear blue sky in which they soar stretches above the buttes, dwarfing the planting scene before me. This farm is such a small part of the universe—and yet—this little bit of prairie is our whole world.

The prairie has defined our lives since the day we arrived here. We are moved forward through time by the seasons of the farm and its crops. We plant seed each spring, tend it during the summer, and hope we have the crop harvested before the last season of the cycle.

Some years farming has paid off; others have been disastrous. Sometimes it was because of our mistakes, and other times it was because of circumstances beyond our control.

It is hard to believe how much we have accomplished in our seventeen years on this farm. We have purchased more land, banking that future crops and cooperative weather will make the payments.

Samuel paid off the final four-dollar filing fee for this claim in '79. He boasts about buying these eighty acres for only a few dollars, but I think we should add the price of pain and sweat.

In 1880 we paid the railroad company $800 for the quarter section across the road to the north of us. It seems as if it has been ours since our homesteading days because that patch of native grass was never plowed. And it may never be. That land is better suited for pasture than farmland.

A year later, we bought another quarter section two miles south and a mile east of here for $2000. It is farther away from the buttes and is better land than the rocky prairie north of us. Oscar turned twenty-two this year and is in charge of that farm. The land will become his when he is ready to marry and start a family.

We hope to have more land by the time Gilbert turns twenty-one in eight years. By the time Samuel reaches seventy, Joseph will be old enough to take over this farm.

I'm confident that our girls will marry and settle nearby. My guess is that they will pick farmers as their mates because they both love the land, too.

And our family and farm will gain another child this year. I don't know if it will be a boy or a girl, but the land will provide for it one way or another.

Of course it is due during fall harvest.

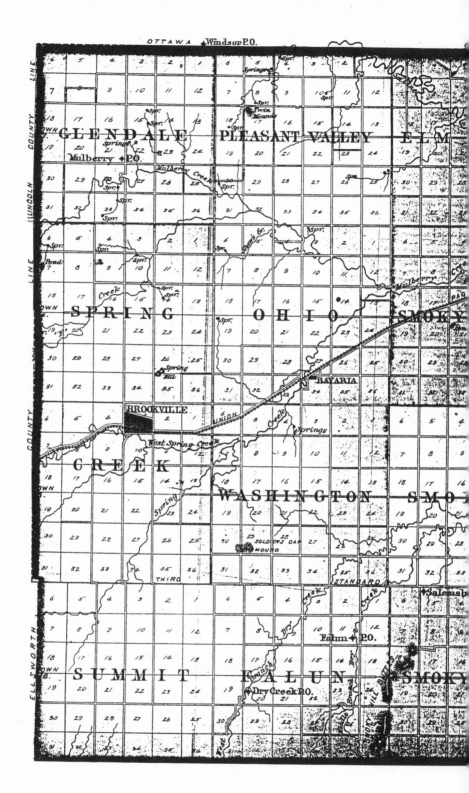

1884- Saline County, Kansas

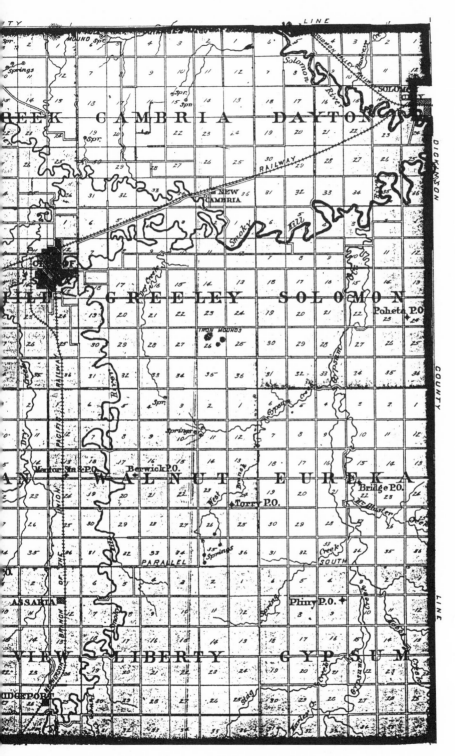

CREEK   CAMBRIA   DAYTON

GREELEY   SOLOMON

WALNUT   EUREKA

VIEW   LIBERTY   CYPSUM

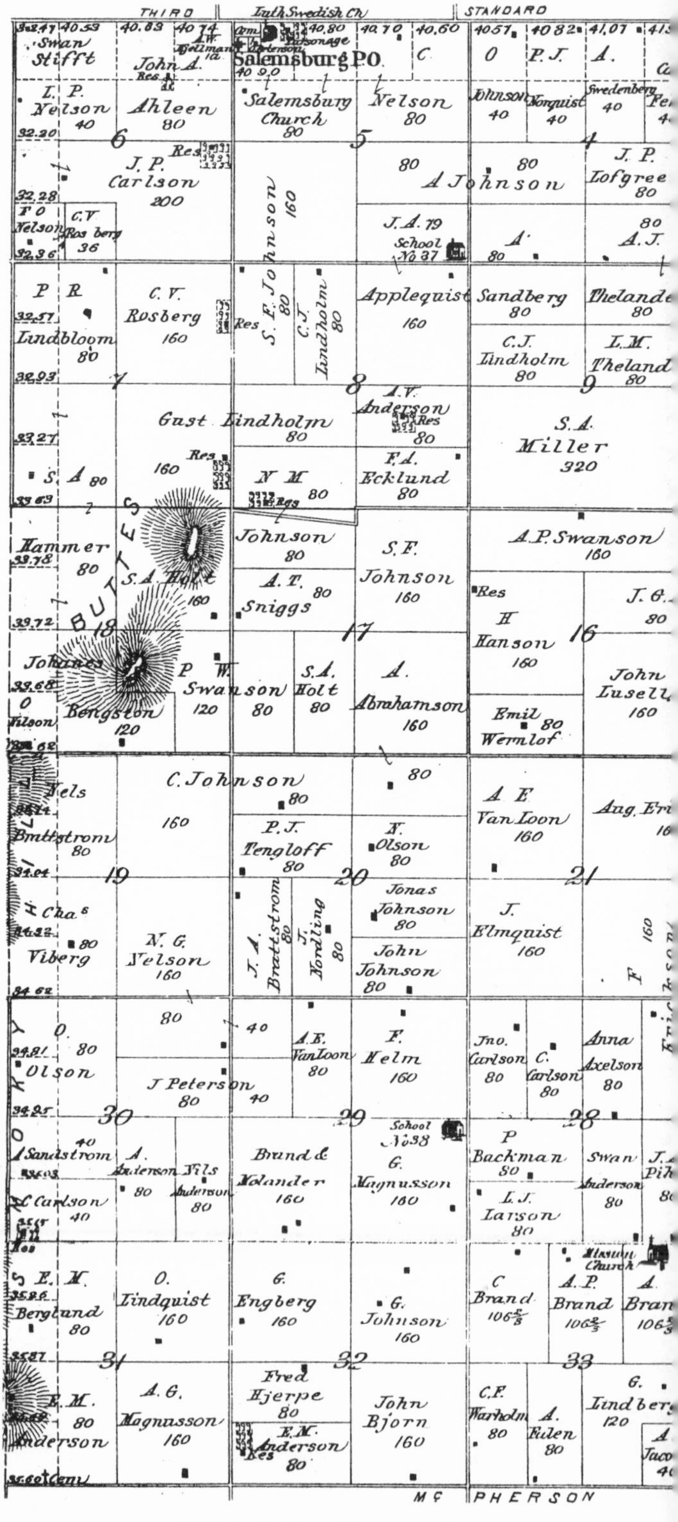
THIRD STANDARD
Luth Swedish Ch
Parsonage
Salemsburg P.O.
Salemsburg Church 80
Swan Stifft
John A. Ahleen 80
L. P. Nelson 40
Nelson 80
Johnson 40
Norquist 40
Swedenberg 40
J. P. Carlson 200
Johnson 160
A Johnson
J. P. Lofgree 80
F O Nelson
C.V. Rosberg 36
J. A. 79
School No 37
P R Lindbloom 80
C. V. Rosberg 160
S. F. Johnson 80
C. J. Lindholm 80
Applequist 160
Sandberg 80
Thelande 80
C.J. Lindholm 80
L. M. Theland 80
Gust Lindholm 80
A. V. Anderson 80
S. A. Miller 320
F. A. Ecklund 80
N M 80
S. A 80
Hammer 80
BUTTES
S. A. Holt 160
Johnson 80
A. T. Sniggs 80
S. F. Johnson 160
A. P. Swanson 160
H Hanson 160
Johanes Bengston 120
P. W. Swanson 120 80
S. A. Holt 80
A. Abrahamson 160
Emil Wernlof 80
John Lusell 160
O Nilson
Nels Brattstrom 80
C. Johnson 160
P. J. Tengloff 80
N. Olson 80
A. E. Van Loon 160
Chas Viberg 80
N. G. Nelson 160
J. A. Brattstrom 80
J. Nordling 80
Jonas Johnson 80
John Johnson 80
J. Elmquist 160
O. Olson 80
J Peterson 80
A. E. VanLoon 80
F. Helm 160
Jno. Carlson 80
C. Carlson 80
Anna Axelson 80
School No 38
Sandstrom 40
A. Anderson 80
Nils Anderson 80
Brund & Nolander 160
G. Magnusson 160
P Backman 80
Swan Anderson 80
L. J. Larson 80
C Carlson 40
Mission Church
E. M. Bergland 80
O. Lindquist 160
G. Engberg 160
G. Johnson 160
C Brand $106\frac{2}{3}$
A. P. Brand $106\frac{2}{3}$
A. Brand $106\frac{2}{3}$
E. M. Anderson 80
A. G. Magnusson 160
Fred Hjerpe 80
E. M. Anderson 80
John Bjorn 160
C. F. Warholm 80
A. Eulen 80
G. Lindberg 120
SMOKY HILL
Mc PHERSON

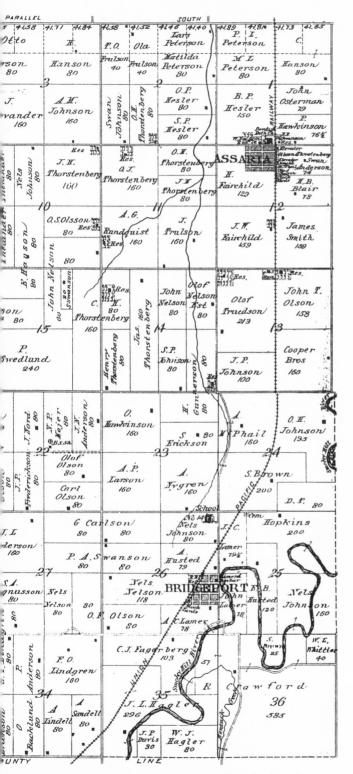

Township 16 South, Range 3 West (Smoky View)

101

This is a plat map with many land parcels and owner names.

...niel | S. | P.L. | S. A. | M. | Gust | Bachant | ...J.

nson | Tharlson 40 | Renard 40 | Brodine 80 | Johnson 80 | Peterson 40 | Sudermar | Tremar 80

Anna wanson 40 | C.A. Danielson Res 80 | S.P. Ringquist 220 | S.G. Mattson 100 | 120 | 80 | Catharine Werry 160

6 | 5 | 4

I.R. Wallace 120

School No.63

Chas Gabrielson 160 | A. Lundburg 120 | Hans Larson 80 | Gabrielson 80 | V.W. Miller 160

John | 7 | W. Johnson 160 | Res | 8 | 9

J.A. Nelson 160 | J.M. Bergquist Res 60 | Aug. Mattson 80 | 40 | Aug. Schultz 160 | Fred Schultz 160

derson 160

lcomb 40 | 80 | C.J. Sjogren Res 160 | John Nelson 240 | K.J. Knutson 160 | C.W. Dopp 160

engren 40 | S. Nordholm 80

18 | 17 | 16

J.P. Johnson 80 | A. Magnusson 80 | John M. 240 | Olof Nelson 160 | P.L. 160

eck | Res

Hannah Frost 80 | C.P. Mattson 80 | Danielson 240 | Gust Ryberg 80 | J.F. Anderson 160 | Res J.P. Anderson 80 | Ci. Aton 80

19 | 20 | 21

J.A. 80 | C.O. Holtman 160 Res | C.A. Sjogren 80 | Gust Holmquist 160 | F. Norburg 160

tman | School 26 2A

berg 80 | C.W. Heggstrand 160 | Gust Holmquist 80 | A.P. Ryden 80 | Chas. Ryden 80 | Res Swan Carlson 80 | A.P. Ryden 80 | J.C. Miller 160 Res

Chas Ryden 80

ank 80 | 30 | Chas Lindstrom 80 | 29 | 28

J.G. 60 | C.A. Johnson 160 Res | P.A. Brown 80 | S.P. Ekland 80 | C.J. Holmberg 80 | C.J. Olson 80 | Ann Carlso Res 80

elson | Swedish Evan. Mission Ch. 80 S.P. | F.O. Holmberg 80

ric 80 | C.J. Brodine 160 | Holmberg 80 | Chas Lindstrom 80 | P.A. Brown 80 | G. Ahlstea 160

und | 160

31 | O.J. | 32 | 33

W. Tharstenberg 80 | 80 | P.J. Carlson 80 | M. Falk | Isaac Swanson

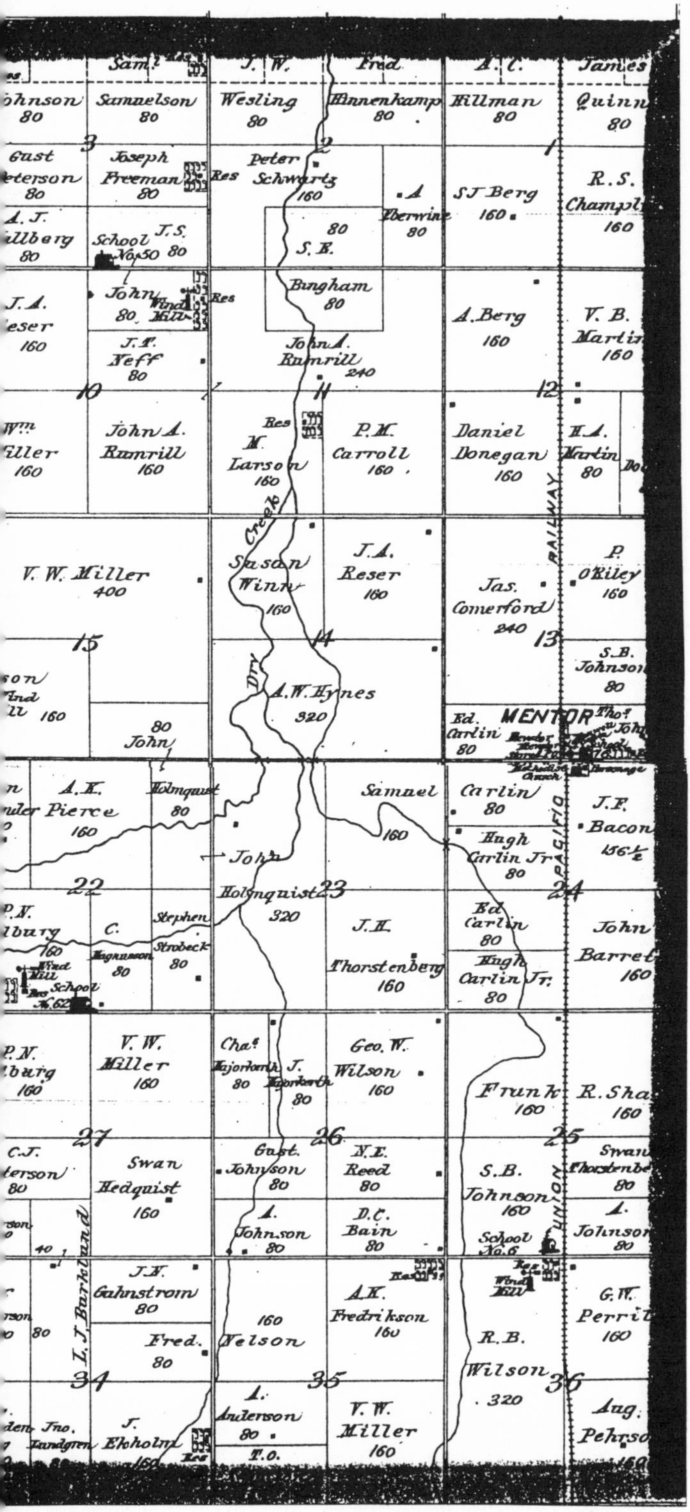

This is a plat map. The following describes the land ownership grid by section.

Top row (partial, sections above 3-2-1):

	Saml...	J. W.	Fred	A. C.	James
...ohnson 80	Samuelson 80	Wesling 80	Hannenkamp 80	Hillman 80	Quinn 80

Section 3:

Gust ...eterson 80	Joseph Freeman 80	Res	Peter Schwartz 160		
A. J. ...illberg 80	School No.50	J.S. 80	S.E. 80	A Iberwine 80	ST Berg 160

Section 2 / 1 area:

					R.S. Champl... 160

J. A. ...eser 160	John 80	Wind Mill	Res	Bingham 80		A. Berg 160	V. B. Martin 160
	J. T. Neff 80			John A. Rumrill 240			

Sections 10 / 11 / 12:

Wm ...iller 160	John A. Rumrill 160	Res M. Larson 160	P. M. Carroll 160	Daniel Donegan 160	H. J. Martin 80	Do...

Sections 15 / 14 / 13:

V. W. Miller 400	Susan Winn 160	J. A. Reser 160	Jas. Comerford 240	P. O'Riley 160
...son Wind M 160	A. W. Hynes 320			S. B. Johnson 80
	John...		Ed. Carlin 80	MENTOR Tho...

Sections 22 / 23 / 24:

...n ...uler Pierce 160	A. K. Holmquist 80	Samuel Carlin 160	Carlin 80	J. F. Bacon 156½
P. N. ...lburg 160	C. Magnuson 80	Stephen Strobeck 80	John Holmquist 320	J. H. Thorstenberg 160	Hugh Carlin Jr 80 Ed Carlin 80 Hugh Carlin Jr. 80	John Barret 160

School No.62

Sections 27 / 26 / 25:

P. N. ...burg 160	V. W. Miller 160	Chas Majorhard 80	J. Thorberth 80	Geo. W. Wilson 160	Frank 160	R. Sha... 160
C. J. ...terson 80	Swan Hedquist 160	Gust. Johnson 80	N. E. Reed 80	S. B. Johnson 160	Swan Thorstenberg 80
...son 40		A. Johnson 80	D. C. Bain 80	School No.6	A. Johnson 80

Sections 34 / 35 / 36:

	J. N. Gahnstrom 80		A. K. Fredrikson 160	Wind Mill	G. W. Perrit 160
...rson 80	Fred. Nelson 80	160		R. B. Wilson 320	Aug. Pehrso...
...den Jno. Langren 160	J. Ekholm 160	A. Anderson 80 T.O.	V. W. Miller 160		

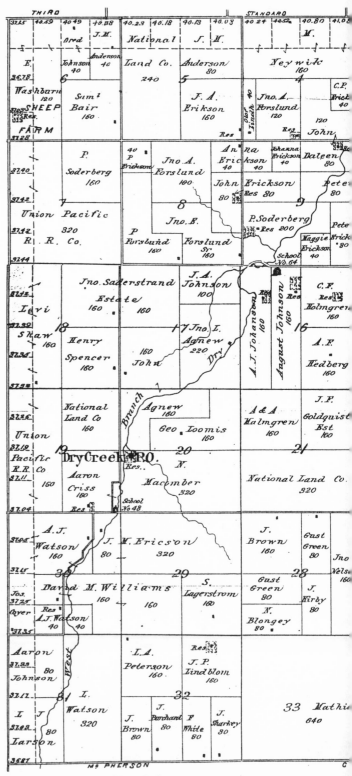

1884- Saline County, Kansas

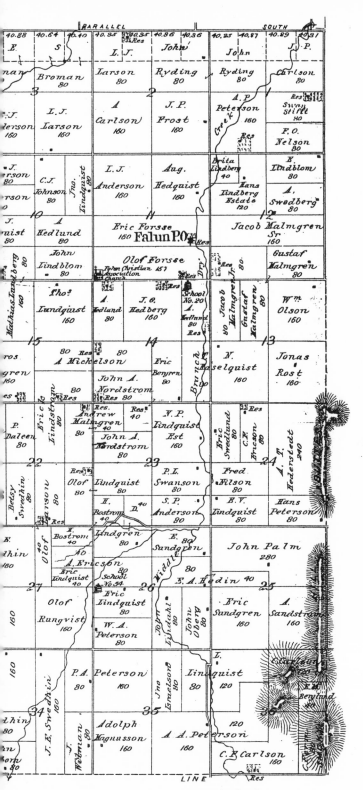

| 40.88 | 40.64 | 40.40 | 40.35 | 40.35 Res | 40.86 | 40.36 | 40.25 | 40.87 | 40.29 | 40.91 |

E. | S | L.J. | John | John | J.P.

nan | Broman 80 | Larson 80 | Ryding 80 | Ryding 80 | Carlson 80

3 | 2 | 1 | Res

A.P. Peterson 160 | Sway Stift 40

J. | L.J. | A Carlson 160 | J.P. Frost 160 | | Res

erson Larson 160 | | | | F.O. Nelson 80

J. | L.J. | Tho. Lindquist 80 | L.J. Anderson 160 | Aug. Hedquist 160 | Brita Lindberg 40 | Lindblom 80

erson 80 | C.J. Johnson 80 | | | | Hans Lindberg Estate 120 | A. Swedberg 80

J. | A Hedlund 80 | Tho. Lindquist 80 | Eric Forsse 160 | Falun P.O. | | 12 | Jacob Malmgren Sr 160

uist 80 | John Lindblom 80 | Olof Forsse 157 | Falun Christian Association Church | Res | | Gustaf Malmgren 80

15 | Tho. Lundquist 160 | A Edlund 80 | J.G. Hedberg 160 | School No.20 A. Edlund 80 Res | Jacob Malmgren 80 | Gustaf Malmgren | Wm Olson 160

14 | A Mickelson 80 Res 80 | John A. Nordstrom Res 80 | Eric Benyrn 80 | Brunck | N. Haselquist 160 | Jonas Rost 160 | 13

P. Daleen 80 | Eric Lindstrom 80 | Res. Andrew Malmgren 40 Res 40 | John A. Nordstrom 80 | N.P. Lindquist Est 160 | Eric Swedlund | C.F. Ericson | Res | A.T. Hederstedt 240

22 | Olof Larson 80 | Res | Olof Lindquist 80 | P.L. Swanson 80 | Fred Nilson 80 | 24

Betsy Swedhin 80 | | H. Bostrom 40 | D. 40 | S.P. Anderson 80 | E.V. Lindquist 80 | Hans Peterson 80

E. hin 160 | Olof 40 | L. Bostrom 40 | Lindgren 80 | Sundgren 80 | E. 80 | John Palm 280

27 | Olof Rungvist 160 | A. Ericson Eric Lindquist 40 | School No.34 Eric Lindquist 80 | Middl | E.A. Hedin 40 | 26 | 25

160 | | W.A. Peterson 80 | John Lindahl 80 | John Oberg 80 | Eric Sundgren 160 | A. Sandstrom 160

160 | P.A. Peterson 160 | Jno Emelson 80 | Lindquist 80 | L. Lindquist 120 | | Benylind

34 | J.E. Swedhin 160 | J. Webman 80 | Adolph Magnusson 160 | A.A. Peterson 160 | 120 | C.F. Carlson 160

Township 16 South, Range 4 West (Falun)   105

| 35.72 | 40.06 | 40.10 | 40.14 | 40.19 | 40.25 Res. | 40.31 | 40.37 | 40.34 | 40.21 | 40.09 | 39 |

C. J. Olson *Spring* Res. 71½
35.77

C. Carlson

C. Carlson 50

C. Carlson 40

Charles Ferm 120

J. Peterson 80

A Jacobson 80

6

5

4

C. Lindberg 80
35.68

O. C. Olson 39½

C. Lindberg 160

P.J. Asplund 80

P. Elving 80

J.G. Bergsten 160

F. Erikson 80

J. Dunn 80
35.89

Olson 40

M. Carlson 30

A.J. Nelson
35.87

M. Carlson 60

Nels Peterson 80

Mrs. M. Anderson 80

School No.10 Res.

P. Larson 80

P. Elving 80

A. Melander 160

D. H.

1

E. Ericson Est. 80
35.75

P. Hedlund 160

8

9

L. Anderson 80

Res. Mrs C. Carlson 80
35.65 35.53

John Wistrand 80

J. Aldrine 80

N.P. Lundquist 80

Andrew Erikson 10

I Anderson 80

Lindsborg Cemetery Assn

O. Erikson 160

Res.

C. Lindberg 40

J Aldrine 40
35.52

G Hoglund 40
35.60

Res. 6 F. Norstrom 160

Res. A. G. Pearson

M. Carlson

LINDSBORG

Swedish Evangelical Lutheran Church 40

J. Christian 100

B.H. Fish 160

13

Gust. Anderson 80
35.68

Oluf Nelson 120
35.76

Res.

O. Newman 48

J.M. Lundbom 40

Wm.Greenfield Res. 60

L.A. Res. Dalin

J.P. Talbot 110

S.Bjorn 80

A.J. Sutton

R.R. Tank

Res.

16

Wm Greenfield 120

J.

A. Johnson 40
35.95

S. G. Johnson 40
36.22

H.Wickstrum 80

Smoky Va Bloy Mill

H.J.P.

Nordlund 7

P.Westman 155

N.J.

Patrick 73½

L.A. Dalin 80

F. Johnson 80

T.J. Mathes 160

19

Gust Johnson 80
36.55

H. Wickstrum 40

Gust.Johnson 40

Westman 113½

Res.

J.F. Johnson 80

Z Wetterstrom

P. Franquist 80

Z.Wetterstrom 80

P. Norberg 80

J.V. John

20

21

Olson 80
36.85

Res.

L.Norberg 80

H Wickstrum 40
37.00

N. Spongberg Est. 80

80

J.Anderson 160

L. Norberg 80

O.G. Peterson 80

Res.

N. Wickstrum 80

A Jen.

J.J. Jenkins 40
37.21

G.Swenson 80

30

30

29

28

N.P. Lundquist 80
37.45

L.N.Holmburg Est. 80

160

John Hall

P. Hendricson 80

P. Norberg 80

C.O. Johnson 80

P.A. Johnson 80

O. Peter

G.W. 30
37.63

Shields
37.68

240

Smoky Hill River

John Hall

P. Henricson 80

A. Hedborn 80

E. Erikson 138

Res.

A.Engstro 104

S. D. 40 Shields
37.52

Shields 40

Res. Rosengren 160

N.E.

N.F. Res 80

Res C.J.Hedborn 80

A.Lindell 80

33

S.Lindell 160

John Lellian 160
37.44

C.Blomberg 80

A. Hedborn 80

A.G. Hendrickson 80

1884- McPherson County, Kansas

Township 17 South, Range 3 West (Smoky Hill)   107

Selected Bibliography

Allender, Etta Wallace. *History of One-Room Public Schools of Saline County, Kansas.* Dissertation for Kansas State University, 1992.

Andreas, A. T. *History of the State of Kansas.* Chicago, Ill.: A. T. Andreas, 1883.

Bartley, Paula, and Cathy Loxton. *Plains Women.* New York: Cambridge University Press, 1991.

Billdt, Ruth. *Pioneer Swedish-American Culture in Central Kansas.* Lindsborg, Kans.: Lindsborg News-Record, 1965.

Billdt, Ruth, and Elizabeth Jaderborg. *The Smoky Valley in the After Years.* Lindsborg, Kans.: Lindsborg News-Record, 1969.

Cordier, Mary Hurlbut. *Schoolwomen of the Prairie and Plains.* Albuquerque: University of New Mexico Press, 1992.

Deaths and Interments- Saline Co., Kansas 1859-1985. Compiled by the Smoky Valley Genealogical Society and Library Inc., 1985.

Dick, Everett. *The Sod-House Frontier 1854-1890.* Lincoln, Neb.: University of Nebraska Press, 1989.

Fite, Gilbert C. *The Farmer's Frontier 1865-1900.* New York: Holt, Rinehart and Winston, 1966.

Habenstein, Robert W., and William M. Lamers. *The History of American Funeral Directing.* Milwaukee, Wisc.: National Funeral Directors of America, Inc., 1962.

Holmquist, Thomas N. *Pioneer Cross.* Hillsboro, Kans.: Hearth Publishing, 1994.

Hurt, R. Douglas. *American Farm Tools from Hand-Power to Steam-Power.* Manhattan, Kans.: Sunflower University Press, 1982.

Lindquist, Emory K. *Bethany in Kansas.* Lindsborg, Kans.: Bethany College, 1975.

————. *The Smoky Valley People: A History of Lindsborg, Kansas.* Rock Island, Ill.: Augustana Book Concern, 1953.

————. *Vision for a Valley: Olof Olsson and the Early History of Lindsborg.* Lindsborg, Kans.: Bethany College, 1970.

Lindsborg Efter Femtio År. Rock Island, Ill.: Augustana Book Concern, 1919.

Lindsborg pa Svensk-Amerikansk Kulturbild från Mellersta Kansas. Rock Island, Ill.: Augustana Book Concern, 1909.

Miner, Craig. *West of Wichita.* Lawrence, Kans.: University Press of Kansas, 1986.

Minnes Album—Svenska Lutherska Församlingen, Salemsborg, Kansas, 1869-1909. Rock Island, Ill.: Augustana Book Concern, 1909.

Peterson, Fred W. *Homes in the Heartland: Balloon Frame Farmhouses of the Upper Midwest, 1850-1920.* Lawrence, Kans.: University Press of Kansas, 1992.

Riley, Glenda. *The Female Frontier.* Lawrence, Kans.: University Press of Kansas, 1988.

Books by Linda K. Hubalek

the *Butter in the Well* series

Butter in the Well

Read the endearing account of Kajsa Svensson Runeberg, an immigrant wife who recounts how she and
her family built up a farm on the unsettled prairie.
  Quality soft book • $9.95 • ISBN 1-886652-00-7
6 x 9 • 144 pages

Prärieblomman

This tender, touching diary continues the saga of
Kajsa Runeberg's family through her daughter,
Alma, as she blossoms into a young woman.
Quality soft book • $9.95 • ISBN 1-886652-01-5
6 x 9 • 144 pages
Abr. audio cassette • $9.95 • ISBN 1-886652-05-8
90 minutes

Egg Gravy

Everyone who's ever treasured a family recipe or
marveled at the special touches Mother added to her
cooking will enjoy this collection of recipes and wis-
dom from the homestead family.
Quality soft book • $9.95 • ISBN 1-886652-02-3
6 x 9 • 136 pages

Looking Back

During her final week on the land she homesteaded,
Kajsa reminisces about the growth and changes she
experienced during her 51 years on the farm. Don't
miss this heart-touching finale!
Quality soft book • $9.95 • ISBN 1-886652-03-1
6 x 9 • 140 pages

(continued on next page)

***Butter in the Well* note cards**— Three full-color designs per package, featuring the family and farm.

***Homestead* note cards**—This full-color design shows the original homestead.

Either style of note card —$4.95/ set. Each set contains 6 cards and envelopes in a clear vinyl pouch. Each card: 5 1/2 x 4 1/4 inches.

Postcards— One full-color design of homestead. $3.95 for a packet of 12.

the *Trail of Thread series*

Trail of Thread
Taste the dust of the road and feel the wind in your face as you travel with a Kentucky family by wagon trail to the new territory of Kansas in 1854.

Quality soft book • $9.95 • ISBN 1-886652-06-6
6 x 9 • 124 pages

Thimble of Soil
Experience the terror of the fighting and the determination to endure as you stake a claim alongside the women caught in the bloody conflicts of Kansas in the 1850s.

Quality soft book • $9.95 • ISBN 1-886652-07-4
6 x 9 • 120 pages

Stitch of Courage
Face the uncertainty of the conflict and challenge the purpose of the fight with the women of Kansas during the Civil War.
Quality soft book • $9.95 • ISBN 1-886652-08-2
6 x 9 • 120 pages

Planting Dreams Series

Drought has scorched the farmland of Sweden and there is no harvest to feed families or livestock. Taxes are due and there is little money to pay them.

But there is a ship sailing for America, where the government is giving land to anyone who wants to claim a homestead.

So begins a migration out of Sweden to a new life on the Great Plains of America.

Can you imagine starting a journey to an unknown country, not knowing what the country would be like, where you would live, or how you would survive? Did you make the right decision to leave in the first place?

Planting Dreams
Follow Charlotta Johnson and her family as they travel by ship and rail from their homeland in 1868, to their homestead on the open plains of Kansas.
Quality soft book • $9.95 • ISBN 1-886652-11-2
6 x 9 • 124 pages

Cultivating Hope
Through hardship and heartache Charlotta and Samuel face crises with their children and their land as they build their farmstead.
Quality soft book • $9.95 • ISBN 1-886652-12-0
6 x 9 • 124 pages

Harvesting Faith
The work and sacrifice of the family's first years on the prairie are reaped in the growth of the family, farm and community.
Quality soft book • $9.95 • ISBN 1-886652-13-9
6 x 9 • 124 pages *(Available Fall 1999)*

Order Form

Book Kansas!/Butterfield Books, Inc.
P.O. Box 407
Lindsborg, KS 67456
1-800-790-2665

SEND TO:

Name _____

Address _____

City _____

State _____ Zip _____

Phone # _____

❑ Check enclosed for entire amount payable to
   Butterfield Books

❑ Visa   ❑ MasterCard   ❑ Discover

Card # ☐☐☐☐ ☐☐☐☐ ☐☐☐☐ ☐☐☐☐

Exp Date ☐☐☐

Signature (or call to place your order) _____ Date _____

ISBN #	TITLE	QTY	UNIT PRICE	TOTAL
1-886652-00-7	Butter in the Well		9.95	
1-886652-01-5	Prarieblomman		9.95	
1-886652-02-3	Egg Gravy		9.95	
1-886652-03-1	Looking Back		9.95	
	Butter in the Well Series - 4 bks		35.95	
1-886652-05-8	**Cassette**: Prarieblomman		9.95	
	Note cards: Butter in the Well		4.95	
	Note cards: Homestead		4.95	
	Postcards: Homestead		3.95	
1-886652-06-6	Trail of Thread		9.95	
1-886652-07-4	Thimble of Soil		9.95	
1-886652-08-2	Stitch of Courage		9.95	
	Trail of Thread Series - 3 books		26.95	
1-886652-11-2	Planting Dreams		9.95	
1-886652-12-0	Cultivating Hope		9.95	
1-886652-13-9	Harvesting Faith (Fall 1999)		9.95	
			Subtotal	
			KS add 6.4% tax	
Shipping & Handling: per address ($3.00 for 1st item. Each add'l. item .50)				
			Total	

Retailers and Libraries: Books are available through Butterfield Books, Baker & Taylor, Bergquist Imports, Booksource, Checker Distributors, Ingram, Skandisk and Western International.

RIF Programs and Schools: Contact Butterfield Books for discount, ordering and author appearances.

Order Form

Book Kansas!/Butterfield Books, Inc.
P.O. Box 407
Lindsborg, KS 67456
1-800-790-2665

SEND TO:

Name _____

Address _____

City _____

State _____ Zip _____

Phone # _____

☐ Check enclosed for entire amount payable to
Butterfield Books

☐ Visa   ☐ MasterCard   ☐ Discover

Card # ☐☐☐☐ ☐☐☐☐ ☐☐☐☐ ☐☐☐☐

Exp Date ☐☐☐

Signature (or call to place your order) _____ Date _____

ISBN #	TITLE	QTY	UNIT PRICE	TOTAL
1-886652-00-7	Butter in the Well		9.95	
1-886652-01-5	Prarieblomman		9.95	
1-886652-02-3	Egg Gravy		9.95	
1-886652-03-1	Looking Back		9.95	
	Butter in the Well Series - 4 bks		35.95	
1-886652-05-8	**Cassette:** Prarieblomman		9.95	
	Note cards: Butter in the Well		4.95	
	Note cards: Homestead		4.95	
	Postcards: Homestead		3.95	
1-886652-06-6	Trail of Thread		9.95	
1-886652-07-4	Thimble of Soil		9.95	
1-886652-08-2	Stitch of Courage		9.95	
	Trail of Thread Series - 3 books		26.95	
1-886652-11-2	Planting Dreams		9.95	
1-886652-12-0	Cultivating Hope		9.95	
1-886652-13-9	Harvesting Faith (Fall 1999)		9.95	
			Subtotal	
			KS add 6.4% tax	
Shipping & Handling: per address ($3.00 for 1st item. Each add'l. item .50)				
			Total	

Retailers and Libraries: Books are available through Butterfield Books, Baker & Taylor, Bergquist Imports, Booksource, Checker Distributors, Ingram, Skandisk and Western International.

RIF Programs and Schools: Contact Butterfield Books for discount, ordering and author appearances.

117

About the Author

A door may close in your life but a window will open instead.

Linda Hubalek knew years ago she wanted to write a book someday about her great-grandmother, Kizzie Pieratt, but it took a major move in her life to point her toward her new career in writing.

Hubalek's chance came unexpectedly when her husband was transferred from his job in the Midwest to the West Coast. She had to sell her wholesale floral business and find a new career.

Homesick for her family and the farmland of the Midwest, she turned to writing about what she missed, and the inspiration was kindled thus to write about her ancestors and the land they homesteaded.

What resulted was the *Butter in the Well* series, four books based on the Swedish immigrant woman who homesteaded the family farm in Kansas where Hubalek grew up.

In her second series, *Trail of Thread*, Hubalek follows her maternal ancestors who travel to Kansas in the 1850s. These three books relive the turbulent times the pioneer women faced before and during the Civil War.

Planting Dreams, her third series, portrays Hubalek's great-great-grandmother, who left Sweden in 1868 to find land in America. These three books trace her family's journey to Kansas and the homesteading of their farm.

Linda Hubalek lives in the Midwest again, close to the roots that started her writing career.

The author loves to hear from her readers. You may write to her in care of Butterfield Books, Inc., PO Box 407, Lindsborg, KS 67456-0407.